The Eccentric and the Quintessential

Boniface & Nkem Ossai

First Edition Published in the United Kingdom in 2016

Second Edition Published in the United Kingdom
in 2022 by aSys Publishing

Illustrations: One Pixel (www.onepixel.com)

Disclaimer

This is a work of fiction. Names, characters, businesses, places,
events and incidents are either the products of the author's
imagination or used in a fictitious manner. Any resemblance to
actual persons, living or dead, or actual events
is purely coincidental.

ISBN: 978-1-913438-63-0

aSys Publishing

This book is dedicated in loving memory of my brother Felix Ossai. Felix will be deeply missed by the whole family.

This book wouldn't have been a success without the effort of my wife, Nkem, who worked tirelessly to ensure the success of this book, not to forget my children Ikechukwu and Ifeanyichukwu.

Finally, a big thanks to my friend Mark Campbell for his immense contribution towards the success of this book.

CHAPTER
ONE

The Interest

It was winter, a cold afternoon with slight showers of rain. John Watson, a 5ft 9" brown-eyed and dark-haired gentleman was looking his best in his slim-fit wool-twill suit and a Belvin Leary wool blend winter coat. He was holding an umbrella above his head as he walked out of the T.M Lewis store along Oxford Circus where he'd just picked up some office shirts.

While he walked to his car, a 5ft 8" tall blonde beauty with blue eyes, in a red Giorgio Armani zip-front ottoman peplum jacket, ran under his umbrella for cover. "Hey, my name is Brenda," she said with a smile. "Can I share your umbrella with you while I wait to catch my bus?" She asked.

John wasn't expecting company, not to speak of a blonde beauty. "Err.., yeah," he said. He adjusted his suit as he tries to comport himself to match the occasion, as well as leave a good first impression. "I'm John and walking to my car," he said. "Oh, where is it?" She asked, as they took steps forward.

His finger pointed forward, "that red Chrysler over there, just the same colour as your dress," said John with a smile.

She turned to John and burst into laughter. "Err, this is becoming interesting," she said. They walked in locked step towards

John's car chatting as if they've known each other forever. Brenda stopped, "let's wait here, my bus will be here in a minute, and I don't suppose you'd agree to give a ride to a stranger," she said. John had quite a busy schedule but he doesn't mind going the opposite direction and wouldn't mind being told off by his boss just to make this stranger comfortable.

Taking an interest in her outfit, John looked at Brenda with admiration, "I like your winter jacket," he said.

This is a "Zac Zac Posen Everly fur-trim zip-front winter coat." There isn't anything special about my jacket, it's just a jacket, John," she said. Interestingly, John continued his line of conversation. "I like your sense of fashion. Your personality and your sense of fashion seem completely fused into one," John said. Brenda seemed to like the admiration and flattery, as she burst into laughter in a manner that sends John a message that he isn't making a fool of himself. "Ha-ha, tell me about it, are you sure about that?" She asked.

"What about we continue this conversation in my car, and where are you headed? I don't mind dropping you off," said John.

"Err, never mind, my office is just a stone's throw away," Brenda replied.

John's emotion is beginning to get the best of him as he's being drawn in by Brenda's beauty. "Hmm, but we haven't introduced ourselves properly. As you know already I'm John, a solicitor, single and still searching," he said. "Are you asking me out on a date? Because you only just met me," Brenda replied.

"I've said nothing, Brenda! I just gave you my profile," John said. Brenda knew the drill and understood that when men say they've said nothing, it implies they've said all there is to say. "She gazed at John and smiled, oh John, I suppose you don't intend to be my future ex-husband?" she asked jocularly. Funnily, the bus took more than a couple of minutes to arrive, this gave the pair an opportunity to explore each other's profile and they chatted away as if they've known each other forever.

"One precedes the other, being your husband comes before being your ex, I guess I'm considered already," he said as his face beamed with smiles. "You've taken the conversation to an interesting dimension. It's nothing, after all, we're two mature adults engaging in a casual and sensible conversation," she said.

"Ok, my friends' call me Brenda, and I work with a real estate firm close to London Bridge, I'm single and wish to remain single until I am convinced," said Brenda.

"Convinced about what? I only gave you my profile but haven't made any proposition," asked John. Even as he tried so hard to make light of his moves, he still wants her to take him seriously as he laughs and continued. "I must confess, those blue eyes of yours at a close range are capable of causing confusion in a man's system," said John.

Brenda smiled, and looked away as she fiddles with her hair. "Oh John, you're making me blush," she exclaimed. John is now unwittingly a captive audience to this beautiful stranger, and he did confess to her that he's captivated by her style as he tries to get her attention. The conversation seems to have moved quickly into those grey areas that kept Brenda on the edge but lucky enough her bus just arrived. "That's my bus," Brenda whispered, pointing towards a bus approaching the bus stop.

"This is my card, said Brenda," as she dips her card into the breast pocket of John's suit. "Can I have yours?" She asked. John hands his card to her. "Hmm, you're so full of life, Brenda. I'll give you a call later today, so we can continue this interesting conversation," said John.

She fixed her gaze on John with a steady smile. "Nice meeting you, John. And make sure you dial me up. Be a good boy, John," said Brenda. She then gave him a peck on his cheek. "Catch you later, Brenda," John replied. She then turned around and John looked on speechless as she inched closer to the bus and boarded the bus, he then waved at her with a beaming smile. John spent a few minutes watching as the bus moved and drove out of sight, particularly reminiscing his encounter with this stranger that stumbled into his path. It was as if he was visited by an angel, and serendipitously, this angel came looking for him.

Immediately Brenda picked a comfortable spot in the bus to sit, she then attempted to put John's card into her handbag, and sadly, the card slipped and fell to the floor of the bus without her knowing.

That night, John got home late from work as usual and rushed to the shower then straight to bed. He then spent some time in bed reminiscing how his day went, and after while in bed, he suddenly got up and reached for the breast pocket of his suit for Brenda's card. He spent some time looking at the card and reading through the granular details in her card, and then reached for his phone because he intended to dial Brenda's phone but then changed his mind almost immediately. Unfortunately, Brenda expected John's phone call that night, but the call never came.

John is a handsome, polished, but an eccentric Englishman with no social life, which explains why his colleagues at the law firm where he works see him as a workaholic and a man without a life who deserves to stay longer at work while others have closed for the day. John's love life has been up and down. His love fantasies can be best described as a fairy tale. He's never into ladies that fancy him, and ladies he likes are usually not interested in him. John's routine is such that he comes home from work very late on weekdays to compensate for the fact that there's no one at home to go to. He does his laundry Saturday mornings and goes out for drinks in the evenings with his work colleagues, Philip and Celine, then goes to church on Sunday mornings.

Brenda, on the other hand, is an American blonde beauty known for her classy lifestyle and for her smile decorated with natural dimples. She's the Broadway kind of lady, with enough sparkle to light up the dormant love life of an unsociable man. She's well mannered, and people find her company interesting because of the warm ambience she carries with her.

The next morning John jumped up from his bed at the sound of the alarm, rushed to the bathroom, got ready, and zoomed off to work. As he walked into the office, "it's 7.45 am and you're late, John," his boss, Tom Bradley, retorted pointing to his wrist watch to remind John what time it is.

"No, I'm not," John replied, as he takes off his jacket and hanged it on the hanger. John wasn't quite perturbed by Tom's frown because he isn't late to work and have resumed much earlier than his colleagues. He considers Tom's yelling to be nothing but Tom's way of jocularly getting under his skin.

Tom Bradley took few steps towards John, with his hand stretched forward towards John. "Where's the paperwork for the insurance contract?" Tom retorted again.

"Which of the insurance contracts?" John asked.

"We are hosting the big guns in the industry and we can't be behind schedule. I mean, Wendy Insurance Plc executives will be here by 9.00am," said Tom.

John wasn't quite pleased with Tom's constant nagging about the time he arrived work, even when he was particularly willing to resume earlier than his colleagues.

John seemed to acquiesce the decision to come to work a bit earlier than his peers, this unwittingly meant that Tom Bradley is now salami slicing John's right to do just as his colleagues, but he now thinks Tom shouldn't take it as a right.

"But 8am is the resumption time and I'm even the first to be here, where are the others?" John asked as he opened his desk drawer, brought out a file and began flipping through the pages of the documents inside the file. Unsurprisingly, Tom tried to make light of the situation to disabuse John's mind of any animosity that's created, and funnily, he isn't much of an actor after all. There's nothing John hates the most like the smug smile on Tom's face each time he tries to patronise him but there's nothing John can do about it. John soon realised that Tom considered him a doss because of his lifestyle that leaves much to be desired.

"Don't worry about the others, John. I know you've got some time to spare, and I'd really love to work with you and use up some of your idle time," Tom replied. Somehow Tom seems to be violating boarders with work as he creeps into John's personal time. In what looked like a light tiff brewing up between the two, John interjected.

"Tom, I know you to be an idealistic person, and I don't think this it's right, but I never mentioned to you I had spare time waiting to be used up, did I?" John retorted. Tom became quite jocular, to avoid bringing out John's gritty side.

"I'm your pal, John. You never told me, I sensed it, and please bring the file to my office," Tom replied.

Tom Bradley turned around and walked back to his office, leaving John alone in the central office as he continued leafing through pages of documents.

Moments later, while John was still going through the files containing the paperwork requested by Tom Bradley, Celine Johnson, a colleague who fancies and has always been sultry around John, walked in, and stood behind John. She then threw her hand around John's shoulder. Interestingly, even when John didn't see who it was that threw her hand around him, he knew it was Celine because the fragrance she was wearing is familiar. More so, it's only Celine that could pull such a sultry stunt with him among his colleagues.

"Hey John, how was your night?" She asked, smiling as she gazed at John whose attention was fixed on the file he was working on.

"Hmm, same same, just another usual cold winter night. Ooh, you smell good, Celine!" John exclaimed.

"I take that as a compliment. But wait a minute, John, you never even bothered to look me up, and why haven't you asked me out? You know I could keep you warm during these cold nights," said Celine.

"Your comment is hypothetical I suppose, and that would be nice of you, Celine. You know you're a beautiful woman," said John, with his attention still fixed on his work.

On hearing this, Celine blushed and gave John a slight kiss on the cheek, leaving stains of lip stick on John's cheek. John stopped his work abruptly and wiped off the stain on his cheek.

"Why did you do that? We're in the office," John protested. "I've been expecting you to take the lead, John. I felt I should show you how to do this," said Celine. John wasn't quite expecting that from Celine, but he isn't unaware that she's into him.

"I only complimented you, Celine. It doesn't mean we're in love and Tom mustn't see you do this," he said. Giving a colleague a peck on the cheek isn't something out of the ordinary, in fact, it's everyday norm, but having her hands around his neck like someone going for a smooch was what got John on the back foot.

"I understand your office sentiment, don't worry, John. Soon, I mean very soon, you'll be mine," Celine said in a seductive tone.

"How do you mean? You and I should remain hypothetical, there isn't any need moving this fairy tale further, and I need to give this file to Tom," said John.

"I know you don't have a girlfriend, so you're stuck with me, baby," said Celine. She then gave John a pat on the back, and then turned around and walked back to her desk. Their conversation then moved away from personal stuff, and morphed into other office matter.

Tom walked into their conversation looking uneasy, the perma-frown on his face speaks volume, he then turned to John and yelled this time. "Where's my file, and I've been waiting all day," he said.

"This is your file, Tom. It's all prepared for your meeting," John replied. Tom collected the file from John and took some steps towards his office but stopped abruptly, and turned around again.

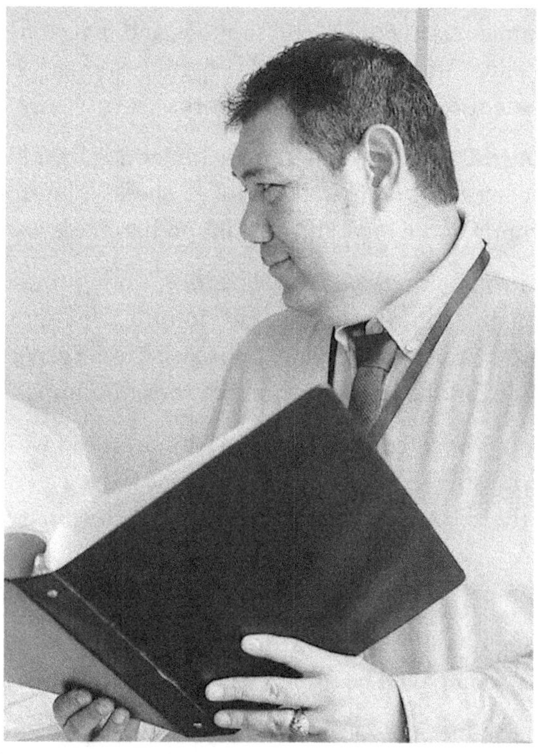

"Join me in the office, John. We've got work to do, and it is going to be a long day," said Tom. Unsurprisingly, John spent all day with Tom securing the insurance contract, and as usual, it's 8pm and John was still stuck in the office when all his colleagues at the office have closed for the day, and gone home. While John remains at the office, a familiar phone call came in from Yorkshire, and this time it's his mum, Maggie.

John checked to see who's calling, and noticed it was Maggie, at first, he hesitated picking up the call, but on a second thought, he shrugged his shoulder and picked the call. "Hello mum," said John.

This time Maggie wasn't quite interested in pleasantries as she hits the nail on the head. "Where are you, John?" she asked in her usual uncooperative tone, suspecting he'll still be in the office.

"I'm right here in the office," John replied. "You mean you're still at work at this time of the night?" Maggie yelled. John isn't unaware that his mum has been keeping tabs on him even though he isn't particularly impressed with his mum's move, he had to engage his mum in this difficult conversation. "Yes Mum, but there are things I needed to tidy up for clients before tomorrow morning," John retorted.

"What about the others, I mean your colleagues, are they still in the office?" She asked in a more subtle tone. Despite the tacky nature of this conversation John made himself an easy audience for his mum, because he's honest to a fault when it comes to telling his mum as it is.

"No, they've all gone, and why are you asking?" John replied.

Maggie adjusted herself as she assumed the critic's seat, and then continued her conversation with John. "The last time I called, you were alone in the office, today it's the same thing, and it has always been the same," said Maggie.

"We handle different clients and there isn't any need for this unfitting comparison, because we handle different clients," John protested. John's response was rather bizarre because he responded in a mumbling tone as he emphasised that time spent in the office shouldn't be of concern to her because it means nothing to him.

John responded in a mumbling tone and told his mum that it doesn't matter how long he stays in the office because it means nothing to him.

"It means a lot, John. Why don't you stop hiding in the office, and go get a life?" She yelled again. John's conversation with his mum was quite odd, as he became agitated and struggled to keep up with his mum's probing conversation. He tried toning things down and suddenly became leery as he told his mum he isn't hiding in the office, and more so, he has a life.

"There's life out there, John, go out and have a life, stop hiding in the office. You're using the office as a veil to mask your weird lifestyle," Maggie exclaimed in a sobering tone.

"Mum, my work isn't a veil and I'm masking nothing, I've told you repeatedly that I'm ok," said John. He went silent on the phone for a while and pleaded with his mum to stop making his life a living hell and after his plea he told her he needed to get off the phone now so he could return to work. Funnily, Maggie isn't willing to let John off easily, not without getting everything off her chest. John now thinks his mum is now intentionally prodding him with her sarcasm.

"You aren't ok, my son. I suppose your hiding in the office hasn't been quite normal and it seems your dad wants to speak with you," Maggie muttered.

John hesitated because having this conversation with his dad is a different kettle of fish, and so, he's been avoiding his dad, particularly when he has an idea of what his conversation with his dad will be centred on. Unfortunately for John, his conversation with his dad leaves him with no room for manoeuvre. "You don't have to bring dad into this, I've to go now," he said. Interestingly, just as John attempted dropping the phone Maggie hands the phone to Jim, John's dad.

"Not so fast, John, you seem to be avoiding me, but I want you to come over this weekend, your cousin will be christening his new-born baby girl," said Jim.

"I don't think I'll have a chance, I've a lot to do at home," said John. Jim gave John the stinker as he accused him of avoiding him at all costs. "I know you won't come," Jim retorted. John protested at his dad's assertion, saying his dad is sounding as if he's a fugitive. Interestingly, John's parents are convinced he treats his work as a form of escapism, and his protest will do little to keep them off his back. His dad wasn't overly friendly this time, and they're needled by a concern that there's something wrong with their son's social life that they just can't put their finger on.

"I suppose you know why, your brother is moving on, and you're stuck in the office," Jim said. "I'm not stuck, dad. I'm at work," John replied.

John left the office 8.25pm that day, when his colleagues at the law firm finished for the day at about 5.30pm at most. As John left the office, he drove straight to a Domino Pizza outlet around Elephant and Castle to get pizza for dinner, after which he drove straight to his house. On getting home, the first thing John did was to play the music of Sonia Spence entitled "Jet Plane", then took off his clothes, went straight to have a shower, after which he opened the refrigerator and brought out a cold can of Diet Coke and began eating his meal for the night. Unsurprisingly, John couldn't get his mind off Brenda while the music was playing, and the thought of Brenda suddenly became overwhelming for him. Somehow, the urge to reach out held him hostage, he decided to call her phone at a point. He then stood up, went into his bedroom, and picked up her card from his bedside where he left it the night before. He brought out his phone to make the call but suddenly developed cold feet and changed his mind again, and went back to dining table with the card in his hand. After his meal that night, as John was clearing the table, he inadvertently cleared the card along with the wrappings for the pizza he just finished eating, and dumped all of it in the bin. He later went to bed with the intention of reaching out to Brenda in a future date.

John just passed his Solicitor's qualifying examination, and decided to invite his friends and colleagues for drink on Saturday evening to celebrate his success. Celine in her usual character, and as she does in her show of support for her colleagues made cake. This cake isn't her regular kind of cake, one thing benign about this cake is that she put so much effort into making this cake. Interestingly, the symbol of a heart boldly displayed in bold red in the middle of the cake got John's friends and colleagues thinking and talking about the unspoken message this cake seems to be passing across. Everyone laughed the moment she uncovered the cake, and that includes John.

They all raised their glasses as they toast to John and his success, but when it's time to cut the cake there was no knife except the wooden knife that came with their meal. Celine quickly suggested they ask the bar staff for a knife, saying she wants the cake to be cut with precision but Lesley on the other hand stressed on her earlier suggestion of using the wooden knife, and insisting that the wooden knife will do the job, because the cake isn't concrete after all.

Celine's persistence meant they'd to get a member of bar staff to get them a knife to cut the cake, and when it's time for John to cut the cake Celine suddenly placed her hand on John's while he cut the cake. Celine sort of stole John's thunder as she seems to have used this moment to register her presence, she didn't consider herself as some kind of small fish in a large pond, she has just positioned herself as the only fish in this pond.

This kind of seems weird and reinforces the unspoken message in the cake, but her cheekiness seems to be sort of enlightening to her colleagues who weren't expecting this from her. John understands what Celine was playing at but went along, laughing. Although, John wasn't naive because he didn't think Celine was stuck on stupid, and as such didn't deny her the niceties that comes with the funny ambience she's creating. Serendipitously, whatever message Celine just passed through the cake meant nothing to John but banter. For all it's worth, Celine wasn't embellishing anything, neither did she in anyway acted frisky, she went about her pursuit of John benignly.

Three weeks later, 4th of February to be precise, was John's birthday. His colleagues at the law firm had planned a small birthday party for him in the office, with Celine assigned the responsibility of managing the entire birthday party. Tom Bradley, who had always taken advantage of John's odd lifestyle, felt this would be an opportunity to compensate John for his selfless and immense contribution to the law firm.

It was mid-day, Tom Bradley alighted from his car and walked through the central office with his hand in his pocket. John smiled as Tom Bradley ambled into the central office and signalled him to come over, but he seemed not to get the message, he then beckoned on him.

"John, meet me in my office," said Tom.

"Ok, you want me in your office right now or when I'm done working on this file?" asked John. "Yes, now, please come with me," Tom replied.

John left what he's doing and followed Tom from behind and opened the door to Tom's office. "Tom, I'm here," said John.

"Tom Bradley continued, Yeah, Friday is your birthday, I suppose, and I want you to know that the office is planning a little something, small get-together to celebrate your birthday, as a way of saying thank you, John, for your contributions to this firm," said Tom.

"Hmm, Tom, I'm lost for words and I don't know what to say. But that's nice of you, thank you, just that I really don't think it's necessary," said John.

"No John, Tom insists. You deserve a thank you, and you can bring your girlfriend if you like," said Tom.

"Ok, ok, thank you, but I don't think having my girlfriend present will be necessary," John replied. Tom pressed on John to bring his girlfriend in, at least to make his birthday party more colourful, but sadly, John had none. "It's your day, John. We are celebrating one our best staff and that'll be an opportunity for me to get to know her," Tom Bradley said emphatically.

"Ok, I'll consider having her around on Friday," John responded as he leaves Tom's office and returned to his desk.

That afternoon, John left the office to have his lunch at a nearby cafe where employees of most of the offices around come for lunch. Not long after John's lunch was served, Celine walked in and met him having beef lasagne, potatoes and vegetables.

"Here you're, John. How does that taste? Celine asked. John nodded his head and smiled in affirmation that the meal he's having tastes so good, but didn't speak because he had just scooped a spoonful into his mouth. Moments later after a successful swallow of what he had in his mouth he was able to speak.

"Hmm, it tastes so nice, why don't you give it a try?" John proposed as he adjusted his seat to make his sitting position asymmetrical to Celine who sat right opposite him and requested for the same menu John was having for lunch.

"This has always been your usual spot in this cafe, I suppose you find it cosy, and like the warmth it provides, but most importantly, their kind of music," Celine said. "Not just the warmth, the lightening and the music creates a kind of ambience that is quite refreshing and helps me to relax after a busy morning," John replied.

Celine takes her first scoop of the beef lasagne and nods. "This taste nice," she said. "I know you would like it, that's why I suggested you go for it and I'm glad you did," said John. They chatted and laughed as they had their lunch. Socialising between this pair kicks off easily because they've this friendship between them that endures.

"That reminds me, I suppose you're aware I'm in charge of organising your birthday party?" Celine asked. John is aware there's a birthday party coming up following his conversation with Tom Bradley, but he'd no clue about who handles what. "Oh, you are!" John exclaimed.

"Yeah, I'm in charge and I suppose you're aware that managing parties falls within my remit," she said, she then leans forward towards John and speaking seductively as she nibbles into his ear. "Now tell me the songs you want to hear at your birthday party?" She asked.

"Ok, 'Jet Plane' by Sonia Spence, 'So Amazing' by Luther Vandross, and 'mind games' by John Lennon," said John. "Is that all?" she asked.

"Yeah, for now, but why're you so sassy about my birthday?" John asked and burst into laughter. "You said what, John? When it comes to you, 'sassy' is an understatement, I could be a lot more than that," she added, as she smiled and gave John a wink.

John reciprocated with a subtle smile and told Celine she never ceases to amuse him, and funnily, Celine leans forward a second time towards John's ear and whispered, saying she will add one more special song to make it four because a song is missing from

John's list of favourites. "What song is it?" John asked. Celine whispered. "Why Fools Fall in Love" by Frankie Lymon, she said. John chuckled and stopped laughing.

"Are you trying to say I'm a fool?" John asked jocularly, but with a stern look. "No, not at all, take that smirk off your face, but you remember that song?" She asked, with a smile on her face.

"Hmm, yeah," John responded with a nod, but still trying to get his head around what Celine is getting at.

Ok, let me help you out here, I mean falling in love is more of a mystery that can't be explained and... John cuts in, and echoed. "Only fools fall in love."

"You see, John, love makes people do foolish things, just as I'm falling for you now!" She exclaimed.

Realising Celine was serious about her feelings towards him, John went quiet and focused on his meal, and moments later Celine decided to change the subject of that conversation when she sensed John is becoming uncomfortable with her expression of her feelings for him.

By the close of work that day, John returned home late as usual and after taking his shower and having his dinner, John lay on the bed enjoying the light music playing at the background. Interestingly, the thought of using his birthday party as an opportunity to get Brenda's attention came to him, but he lacks the nerve to make the move of reaching out to her just because she seems too classy for him. Moments later, he rolled over to the other side of the bed and reached out to his bedside drawer for Brenda's card, since that's the only way he could get in contact, but the card wasn't there. Then he got off the bed, turned on the light and searched every nook and cranny of his apartment, yet he couldn't find the card either. He then returned to bed with a deep feeling of disappointment. John suddenly became depressed because he suddenly felt this overwhelming heaviness as he realised Friday's birthday isn't just any other birthday party but one that will expose the emptiness of his social life. What a crazy world he thought to himself and muttered, saying Brenda should have been here to take this heaviness away. He stood up again from bed walked towards the window and opened the window slightly to allow some fresh air through, to see if the freshness of the air will provide some relief, he then returned to bed and continued reminiscing the few minutes he spent with Brenda.

Even as he lay in bed facing up, he suddenly focused on the night sky through the tiny space between the curtains in his window that allowed him a peek at the night sky that suddenly seemed closer to him than usual. He then focused on a particular star whose light twinkles in a manner that fascinates him. He imagined the star to be Brenda and watched for a while as if the star was communicating to him in coded language, and even though Brenda isn't within reach the star seems to leave quite an impression, and a feeling in John that makes him feel Brenda's heart is within touching distance. After a while of his inability to make a sense of it, he winked, turned over as if there's this sudden rush of sleep that came upon him, and in a matter of seconds he fell asleep.

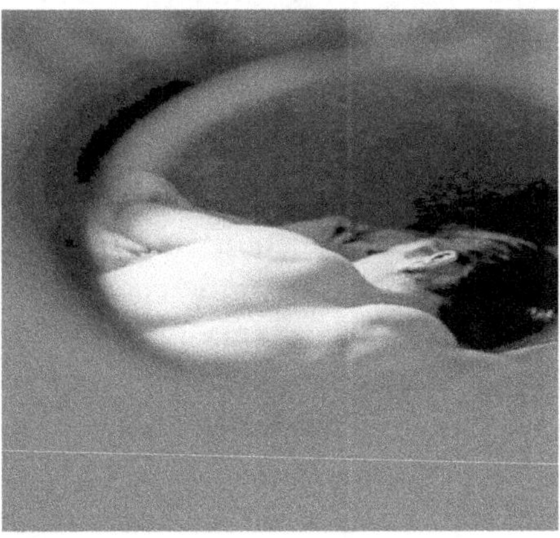

The moment Brenda set her eyes on John she seems to know right away that this is the man she has been waiting for, though, she couldn't fathom how, but deep down she knew this is the guy.

She immediately had this pretty picture of herself and John together right in her head. But now that they have both serendipitously lost their only means of reaching out to each other, it means Branda's thought about herself and John is nothing but a mere figment of her imagination, or maybe they aren't actually meant for each other. She couldn't help it but asked herself, what on earth happened to John's contact card she kept in her handbag that made her unable to reach out to him, yet was mad at the fact that John didn't reach out either. She then muttered to herself again saying maybe he isn't interested after all, because she associates reaching out to being interested. She thought providence brought this guy her way but she isn't sure anymore. John on the other hand wondered what happened to Brenda's card in his possession, and he's equally torn apart by the fact that Brenda didn't reach out and felt maybe she isn't interested after all.

It's John's birthday, and Tom Bradley allocated two hours after the close of work, 4.30pm to 6.30pm for John's birthday party. Some clients dear to the law firm joined in the get-together.

While John stood by the corner with one of the clients in attendance chatting as the light music at the background created a warm and friendly ambience.

Tom Bradley walked into the conversation and turned to John, "where's your girlfriend, is she on her way?" He asked. John quickly wriggled himself out of this situation with an excuse and said his girlfriend can't make it and she won't be coming. Tom seems not to be having John's excuses suggesting it isn't too late to bring his girlfriend in, as he brought out his phone to speak to and convince John's girlfriend to come over. "This is your day, John. You mean there isn't anyone joining you for the party, no girlfriend, no friend and family member?" asked Tom.

"Ooh, Tom, I'm ok, don't worry about that," John said as he tries to assure Tom that he's fine and urged him not to push it. "Ok, if you say so," Tom responded and put his phone back into his pocket, then turned around as he tries to get the attention of the crowd.

Listen up everyone, one, two, go. Everyone sings on Tom's count. He's a jolly good fellow, he's a jolly good fellow, and he's a jolly good fellow which nobody can deny. They all cheered and jeered as the party kicks off.

Tom Bradley continued, "Today, this law firm is celebrating a man who has given so much to this firm, and this is our own little way of saying thank you to John Watson. "For all it's worth, I understand the frustration when you think you're taken for granted, and I just want you to know you aren't taken for granted, and I want to say a big thank you," said Tom.

After his speech, Tom paused and asked, if anyone has something to say.

Happy birthday mate, you're a great guy to work with and you deserve to be celebrated," said Philip.

"Happy birthday, John, you've been a wonderful colleague and we love you, please be happy and have fun," said Lesley.

"Happy birthday, honey, you look so lovely today," said Celine as she kissed John on the cheek while Philip and others present looked on and smiled with some amusement.

"Ok, let's have a toast," Tom Bradley proposed. They all raised their glasses of wine ready for the toast to John.

Wait, wait, said Celine as she tries to get everyone's attention, immediately after the toast. She put on the music of John Lennon titled 'Mind games,' then Luther Vandross titled 'So Amazing' followed by 'Jet Plane' by Sonia Spence. While the music continued to play, the staff of the law firm and their guests in attendance spent some time socialising, and after a while Tom Bradley called to get the attention of everyone. It didn't take long the chatting stopped as they were all ears waiting to hear what Tom had to say, he then proceeded to inform them that if anyone has anything for John, it's time to give it to him. Tom Bradley brought out a pack of an expensive white leather DKNY wristwatch and gave it to John. He continued, "Once again, I just want to say thank you, John," said Tom.

"This is for you, mate," said Philip as he handed John a striped red tie and a bottle of champagne.

"John, this is for you," said Lesley, as she handed him a book titled '*The Great Minds*' and a bottle of red wine.

"Honey, today is your day, and I'm proud of you," Celine said as she gave John a complete set bespoke suit, and a bottle of red wine. Funnily, Celine has a way with John in her usual organic display of affection, and even as he tried keeping up appearance not to make her feel unwanted she became jocular with him. This is because she thinks his smile obligates him, yet he's disillusion by her expression of interest in him.

"Thank you, thank you, this is becoming more interesting, I told John to bring his girlfriend, so she can see how much we love John, unfortunately she couldn't make it," said Tom Bradley.

Celine cuts in while Tom was still speaking, "I'm here, and I've seen how much you all love him," she said with a smile. Funnily, Celine's comments came as a surprise to Tom, and it got him all riled up, and he quickly interjected. "Is it you!"

Philip didn't hesitate to diffuse any suspicion in Tom's mind as he quickly chided her to stop being so theatrical. "No, I'm not, and I suggest you don't think otherwise," Celine insists. Yet, Tom Bradley was a taken aback and became curious as Celine fawned over John, but decoding the thread holding these two together might prove difficult.

Philip continued, "Tom, I think she's just kidding," said Philip. "I suppose so," Tom interjected. It's now blindingly obvious that Celine's showy display of courtly love towards John is now common knowledge among his colleagues, particularly with this brave move.

Celine is a paragon of virtue and kindness, who would rather not vegetate in the dark, and remain behind the scene but embrace the limelight whenever the opportunity presents itself. Even as they all relish the light music simmering at the background, Philip gave John a wink urging him to be careful not to toy with Celine's heart, lest he relish Celine's venom.

The warm ambience continued as they sip from their glasses of wine while they all engaged in a chat, John was chatting with Tom and Philip, while Celine was chatting with Lesley and two clients of the law firm who decided to join in the party. Suddenly the song 'Why Fools Fall in Love' began to play. Immediately, John turned to Celine from where he was, and established eye contact, she then winked her eyes at him and smiled. For all it's worth, this isn't just any party, this is an opportunity for Celine to join hearts with John, and this gesture is more like a dressing room rehearsal for Celine.

Arguably, Celine's wisdom is something to be cherished, and sadly, she isn't one to be taken for granted because of her benignity.

Moments later, while holding a glass of red wine, John walked up to Celine while she was alone, they chatted for while, but while they had their conversation, John asked a question of interest. "The suit, I never told you my size, how come you know?" asked John. Celine unwittingly burst into laughter. "I know things, and

I know a little about you, John. Where your treasure lies, your heart will be also, you remember?" Celine asked.

"Are you implying I'm your treasure?" John asked.

"Of course yes!" Celine exclaimed in a whisper. You worth much more than gold to me, she echoed further.

"This is becoming more interesting, and I suppose your assessment of my worth is an exaggeration," John said with a smile.

Celine took advantage of the friendly ambience coupled with the influence of alcohol to make her first bold move. She looked into John's eye and told him she doesn't mind coming over to his place tonight, or him coming over to hers, maybe she can make today special for him.

Celine isn't belligerent and neither is she illusory to think that because the sun looks small from a distance she could pass her hands around the sun and squeeze it like a ball. She's obviously marshalling out her plans, and she's keen to see it through.

It's arguably obvious that John might get more than he bargained for this day, because Celine might be more than a handful, and it's unlikely that she will give John the opportunity to make a run for it.

John understands quite well, what Celine was playing at, and even if dragged by the collar, John seems unwilling to drink this Kool-Aid in whatever form it's presented. He'd rather scream blue murder, than go along with this subtle invitation that seems quite tempting.

Interestingly, Celine smiled and gave John a pat on the back immediately after throwing the bait at him. "I appreciate the kind gesture, but not today, let's not dampen the mood of this lovely moment," said John.

Celine pushed further, as she tried to persuade John she would come over to his place just for a cup of coffee, but John has been around the block a few times and knows the drill. He didn't hesitate to let Celine know it isn't just a cup of coffee, he laughed to make things light as he remained courteously civil, but told her it always starts with a cup of coffee but ends with something different.

"Why're you vehemently denying the fact that you're in love with me?" Celine protested.

"That's hypothetical, I guess, and I suggest you talk about this in a nuanced manner," John retorted.

"When else will it be, if not a day like this when the atmosphere is perfect?" Celine asked.

"I never planned for company tonight, it will be me just being by myself, I call it my 'me moment'," said John.

"Whatever you call it, John. Me time, or me alone time, it's just not right. People don't stay alone by themselves, we are social animals, remember?" said Celine.

As Philip seeks to get everyone's attention, he cuts in while Celine was drowned in a conversation with John. "Guys, guys, John wants to say something," said Philip.

Celine whispered into John's ear, "did you request audience?" she asked. "No, not at all, you know Philip has got some tricks up his sleeve, maybe this is one of them," said John. "Say something, then," said Celine as she taps John on the shoulder. John turned around and began addressing his host and guests. Funnily, John was quite emotional with the expression of love received from his colleagues. He took to the centre of the gathering to make a speech.

"I want to thank you all for making me feel this special, and I must confess that I'm short of words to express how I feel. "Tom, thank you." He then turns to Philip, "mate, thank you." And to Lesley, "thank you, Lesley, you look great, thank you." Then to Celine, "Celine, thank you for making today worthwhile," and finally, facing the clients that were present, "thank you so much."

That day Celine didn't come with her car to work, though, it was a deliberate act. As the get-together wraps up, she asked John to drive her home, and when they arrived at Celine's house, she began engaging John in a long conversation and John's entire attempt to make Celine summarise her conversation was futile. After a while John began showing signs of frustration. "Celine please, it's getting late, get down and go home," said John.

"John, it's Friday, I'm spending the night in your place, why don't you just turn the car around and we go over to your place?" Celine asked. John is now in a bind, and all efforts to wriggle out of Celine's grip seems to be falling apart like a pack of cards. "As I said earlier, I've got no plans for company tonight," John replied.

"Don't tell me you were serious about your "me moment", that doesn't make sense. John, please reverse the car, and let's go to your house," Celine said with a smile. Sadly, Celine is now more unwittingly determined to get John, particularly because he's playing catch me if you can with her, and she isn't a fan of people playing hard to get but John's case is the opposite, now that her sights are set on John.

"Why are you doing this to me?" John asked, with a feeling of frustration. "Don't tell me you're afraid of a lady," she replied. "Of course, not!" He exclaimed.

John loosened his tie a bit to give room for some allowance which implies his exasperation. "Then why are you looking so tense? It isn't proper to keep a lady waiting," Celine protested.

"Ok, you won, and it means you're spending the night in my house," John said, as he reversed his car and left for his place. The friendly and warm ambience returned after the tense few minutes.

"I find you to be quite impressive, and maybe not too charming, but always unassuming," said Celine.

"How do you mean?" asked John.

"I know you, John, you've got skills," she said and smiled. Moments later, John stopped the car in the front of his usual Domino's Pizza outlet to get pizza. "Excuse me, I'll be back in a couple of minutes," he said.

Celine didn't hesitate to ask John, what it was and why he's stopping the car. "I just want to get pizza. I'll be back in a minute, and do you've any preference?" John asked. Interestingly, she told him she just left a birthday party and has been snacking all along, and funnily asked John if he still needs to eat dinner.

"This isn't a proper dinner, but something to snack on when we get home, do you've any preference?" He asked again.

She jocularly told John she has always had preferences, but in this circumstance, she's having the same thing as him. She then added a little banter as she suggested to John that it's time they start liking the same thing since they're now inadvertently becoming two peas in a pod. Minutes later, John joined Celine in the car and they drove off. "Hmm, this dish smells nice, the aroma is inviting," said Celine. "That's expected, and I suppose you'll be tempted to go for a slice," John said.

And moments later they arrived at John's apartment, and John didn't hesitate to receive Celine officially into his home. "Welcome to my house," said John. "You don't need to welcome me into your apartment," Celine replied. "I know this apartment, and this apartment need's a woman," she said, then turned to John and asked what he thinks about her comment.

John has a healthy appetite for classy ladies and the fact that he considers himself middle income earner implies he equally has a fairly healthy pocket. Unfortunately his healthy pocket has not brought him the kind of woman his appetite craves.

Celine on the other hand isn't doing anything covert, her actions are overt all along, without making allowance for any plausible deniability of her intentions, and John knows it. Arguably, Celine isn't some kind of ugly cow that's classless, John just has this perception of her as a sister and friend sort of, and that's where he drew the line, yet that didn't stop her from continuously wagging John's tail.

She didn't particularly like the fact that John has made the word love to be an overrated phenomenon, but this time she's covertly urging him to open his eyes and grab what's right before him and make the best out of the present than dawdling and waiting for a future relationship that might never be. Since John remained mum, and didn't respond to Celine's comment, Celine continued her tour of John's living room, and then stopped suddenly before throwing the question to John for the second time. "This apartment needs a woman, what do you think?" She asked.

John is undeniably a self-conscious person who seems to have surmised Celine's move, yet pretended to be illusory about what Celine was about and the direction she's headed.

Ok, I'll think about the needs of my apartment, and I'll take your comments under advisement, but for now, red wine, champagne, and brandy, what do you care?" John asked.

Celine hesitated but later told John they've taken enough red wine at the birthday party, and suggests they go for champagne. As John heads for his wine bar, he turned on the TV and puts on the movie titled 'You May Not Kiss the Bride'.

"Oh, I've watched this movie a couple of times, it'll be nice watching it again, but why this movie, are you learning the tricks of how not to kiss your bride?" Celine asked. Interestingly, John quickly put things into the proper perspective as he told Celine that the bride in this case is hypothetical and the kiss itself is metaphorical. "There isn't any need indulging ourselves in hypothesis and metaphor, I'm right here with you just kiss the bride, John!" She exclaimed. John burst into laughter, as he sets the table and said, "Let's eat," but Celine is more forward thinking than John that's focus on the now. "Let's toast to happiness," said Celine.

They both lifted their glasses of champagne and made a toast to happiness, and to the future.

After eating, John showed Celine to the bedroom, but she rushed into the shower first for a quick shower, after which John gave her one of his T-shirts and combat short to change into, before she joined John again in the living room to continue the movie.

After watching the movie, Celine went into the bedroom to sleep, expecting John to come to bed, but he stayed back and decided to sleep in the living room. Celine felt disappointed and stayed awake for a while to see if John will eventually join her but decided not to press further when he failed to turn up. The next morning, while Celine was still asleep, John made breakfast of toasted bread, poached eggs, hash browns, sausages, and bacon, with a cup of tea by the side.

He immediately walked into the bedroom where Celine was still asleep but not fast asleep, "Breakfast is ready!" John exclaimed.

"What? Don't tell me you've been cooking?" she replied.

"Yeah, you want your breakfast served on the dining or served here in the bedroom, what's your pleasure?" John asked.

Interestingly, this is an opportunity for John to hone his culinary skills. "It has been long since I got this kind of special treat, you're full of surprises and I like it," said Celine.

John tried as much as he could to make Celine's stay a memorable one, at least to compensate for the awkward moments of the previous night, as he avoided getting into something romantic with her.

"A lady deserves to be treated well," John replied. Celine couldn't help but express her heart felt emotion because John's hospitality is nothing short of a show of affection and love. She didn't hesitate to spell it out for what it is, as she told him he has made her feel like a princess, but didn't hesitate to inform John she would join him at the table, but needed to freshen up first.

"Ok, there's mouthwash in the bathroom," said John.

"You remember I told you earlier that I find you very impressive, and unassuming?" asked Celine.

John subtly tried to keep things within a platonic frame, and quickly told her they had lot of drink the night before, and a nice breakfast will be the best thing to break the fast.

"You've got skills, you know. This is one of them, but it is the least of them, I suppose," Celine said with a smile.

"You mean there are other skills?" John asked.

She cynically pulled John's leg as she jocularly told John he has refused to show his skills to her, that was why he chose to sleep on the couch last night. "At least you've seen one. Maybe one day, you'll see another, I suppose," John replied.

After eating her breakfast, John went on to do his laundry, while Celine went to the bathroom, took her bath, dressed, and got ready to go.

Celine chatted with John while he does his laundry as she waited for him to finish up and drop her off at home. John unwittingly hurried up and left his flat with Celine as he walked her to his car for a ride to her place.

John drove Celine to her house. "Thank you John, I had a great time last night, it was fun," Celine said, as they arrived at her house. "You're welcome," John replied. Sadly, Celine didn't want to leave without expressing her disappointment as per the one thing that was lacking in John's hospitality. "But one thing is missing," Celine retorted. "What, what's it?" John asked.

She looked at John, eye ball to eye ball, and told him he knew what it is, and it would've been a perfect night if he'd slept in the bedroom. She then burst into laughter, yet thanked John for the company, for the previous night and acknowledged it was fun.

"You're welcome," said John. "Oh, let's do this another time," Celine said, as she steps out of the car and gave John a peck on the cheek.

CHAPTER
TWO

Providence

It was 12.20pm on Sunday afternoon. John just left St. Paul's cathedral and drove straight to Tesco supermarket to buy some groceries for the week. Interestingly, Brenda just finished shopping in the same supermarket, and was on her way out of the supermarket. Serendipitously, while on a downward-moving escalator Brenda spotted John in the opposite direction going upward.

She couldn't wait to exit the escalator which she eventually did, as she hurriedly left the escalator, turned around and stepped into the upward moving-escalator in her attempt to catch up with him.

"Hey John, John, is that you?" She asked, with a smile. John turned around to see who it was that's calling and there was a flicker of recognition and his eyes were as wide as saucers in excitement. "Oh my God, Brenda, is that you?" John asked, feeling so ecstatic. "Of course, it's me!" She exclaimed.

John drew closer to Brenda, and didn't stop short of giving her a big hug. He was like a child that just found his most cherished toy that was thought to be lost. "It's been a while, and there's not a day that goes by that I don't think of you," said John.

"I expected your call but you never did, and if you missed me this much, why didn't you call me?" Brenda asked. Their previous encounter was brief yet there was a connection between the pair and despite the space and time between them, the spark is still not missing in their second encounter.

"That's my bad, and I must confess I messed up, but you should've called as well, Brenda," John said, with smile.

"Sure, I should've, but somehow I lost your card in the bus, I just can't explain how," she replied.

"Hmm, I'm so sorry, and I thought you were just joking about catching up," said John.

"Now that we found each other, it's an opportunity to start afresh, so, what's up?" she asked.

"I just want to pick up some groceries, before heading home, what about you?" asked John. With smiles on both of their faces, John's life is about to unravel in a dimension he'd only dreamt of because his work life is obviously weaved into the distinct areas of his social life and all that is about to change.

Interestingly, the pair has a lot to say to each other particularly now that providence gave them a second chance as they cross paths for a second time. Brenda quickly offered to walk John through the aisles and help him out with his shopping. She then held John by the hand as they walked through the aisles chatting away as if they've been lovers forever.

An hour later, they finished shopping and stepped into the downward-moving escalator on their way out. "Let's go to your house," Brenda said, as they walked towards the car park.

"Hmm, yeah, yeah, but I hope you aren't afraid of heights because I live on the 15th floor of a sky-rise building," John replied. Interestingly, the pair has a lot in common that meets the eyes.

"Err, why the hesitation, and are you trying to scare me?" Brenda asked. "Of course not," said John.

"I live on the 12th floor and yours is the 15th floor, so why should I be afraid of heights?" asked Brenda.

As they got to the car park, "that's my car," Brenda said, pointing at a red Chevrolet.

"Hmm, how come we both own red cars and live in sky-rise buildings?" John asked, bursting into laughter.

John couldn't help but agree with Brenda that they've got a lot more in common than she knew about, Brenda then asked John to drive while she follow him from behind. They both got into their cars, but immediately Brenda got into her car she took off her jacket, then turned on the ignition. John took the lead and Brenda followed John from behind. Moments later they arrived John's place, John first got out of his car and went to help Brenda out of hers, she held John by the hand immediately they got out of the elevator. As they walked towards John's apartment in locked step, John was holding a book he picked up from his car, along with the bag of groceries he bought at the supermarket in his other hand.

"What book is that?" Brenda asked.

"Err.., this book? This is a bible," said John.

"Seriously, the bible, you mean you're a Christian?" she asked, curiously. "Yeah, I just left church before we met at the super-market," John replied.

Brenda told John her parents are Christians and they taught her values the Christian way, just that she embraced the liberal values and just don't go to church.

"Welcome to my place," John said, as they both walked into John's apartment. Within minutes of stepping into John's apartment, she quickly made a brief assessment of John's place as her eyes ran through the four corners of John's apartment even as she stood in one spot. "Hmm, yeah, you've got a nice place," said Brenda. She then walks to the window, to catch a view of the surrounding streets as she looks down through the window. John walked towards her and stood charismatically by her side to see what it is that caught Brenda's attention.

Brenda stood statue-still by the window and was speechless for a while and suddenly turned to John. "For the record, John, I'm not a cheap woman. A lot of guys have shown real interest in me but I don't fancy them, and I'm not everyman's woman. I'm not dating anyone but I can't explain why I had an interest in you from the very first time I set my eyes on you. Though, you're yet to convince me," said Brenda with a smile.

"Thank you for making the effort," John replied, as he stood right by her side, looking down at the streets through the window with her.

"Seriously, John! Why're you saying this?" Brenda retorted.

John didn't hesitate to confess to Brenda that he had an interest in her from the moment she stepped under his umbrella, just that he lacked the balls to make the move.

"Why? All you need to do is just make a simple move," Brenda said with emphasis.

"That's my bad, and I thought you weren't serious the other day. I felt you would turn me down," said John. "Are you afraid of rejection or what?" Brenda asked.

John reminded Brenda he has been dealing with rejection all his life, yet not all women reject him. "How do you mean?" Brenda asked.

John smiled, holding Brenda's hand as he told her it's only the classy ladies that reject him and funny enough she has got style, and that increases the possibility of rejection.

"Wow!" Brenda exclaimed. "A lot of ladies fancy me actually, but I'm only attracted to the classy ones, just that these classy ladies aren't into me," John said.

"How do you rate me, then?" Brenda asked.

"You belong to the classy, which was why I was afraid you would turn me down. Hmm, pardon my manners. What do I offer you? I've got champagne, red wine, and brandy," asked John.

How come you got these varieties? Brenda asked, as she expressed surprise because John doesn't actually look like the drinking type of man. "Actually, I drink, but I drink alone, which explains how lonely my life has been," said John.

"I like your sense of humour, but don't make it look like you're some sort of a loser," Brenda said, laughing hysterically.

John jocularly told Brenda that he's unlucky as those that come his way are actually those he doesn't fancy. "Funny enough, those I want don't want me, and it kind of makes me look like a man playing the loser's game," he retorted.

"Ok, ok, just give me red wine, let's savour this moment," said Brenda. She reached for her glass of red wine when John eventually offered it to her.

So they continued with their catching up and interestingly, John didn't hesitate to seize the moment to make the move as he told

Brenda she's exactly what he has hoped for all his life as he hands her the glass of red wine. He continued, saying she's classy, she's is hot, he doesn't know her much, but she'll be fun to be with and he's already emotionally entangled with her.

"What, seriously!" Brenda exclaimed.

"Actually, God just answered my prayers today. This moment means a lot to me, and frankly, I'm blown away by your personality. "What, am I your answered prayers?" Brenda asked, and burst into laughter.

"I prayed to God to end my loneliness, and to give me a second chance with you. And just after church, I met you," John said with a smile. "So you call this fate?" Brenda asked.

"Yeah, sort of," John replied. Brenda sounded a note of caution and reminded John they're still strangers to each other, meaning they knew nothing about each other. John drew closer to her and they held hands, he turned around and fixed his gaze at her and responded.

"What about fate? Our hearts seem to be strangely knitted," asked John.

Brenda wants to take things slowly, so they could get to know each other as things progresses, and fate shouldn't be confused with stupidity. She then told John she's still sceptical, and handing her heart to a stranger in the name of fate could be a risky venture.

John interjected and he reminded Brenda of the saying, "always give a stranger a chance, because if you don't they'll always remain a stranger."

"Then let's toast to the future and to a stranger, but we will have to take things slowly," Brenda said as she points her finger at John.

"You mean slow?" John asked, rhetorically.

"Yeah, one step at a time, so we know what works and what doesn't," said Brenda.

"Hmm, I'm cool with that," John replied.

After the toast she sat on the couch to make herself comfortable, while he turned on the TV, and sat opposite her as they relished their glass of wine. John then promised Brenda a tour of his apartment in her next visit. "Ok, but why not today?" she asked.

Worried about the state of his apartment, John held Brenda in abeyance as he wasn't comfortable showing Brenda around because he didn't have time to tidy his apartment to be fitting of a host expecting an important guest.

"Hey, don't worry, I have my reasons, but I'll do that on your next visit," said John.

"When do you intend to return my visit? In my case, I'll give you a tour of my apartment," she said with a smile.

John jumped at the offer with his eyeballs wide open, she then said it will possibly be next weekend, but she doesn't mind him visiting before then, if that won't sound creepy.

Brenda was quite upfront about John's visit, as she assured him there isn't anything creepy about his decision to pop into her place even before the scheduled weekend visit. "You're just ecstatic and that's the mystery of emotional entanglement, and what's your special song?" she asked.

'So Amazing' by Luther Vandross, 'Mind games' by John Lennon, 'Jet Plane' by Sonia Spence," John replied.

For me, I would say, "The Best Things in Life Are Free" by Janet Jackson and Luther Vandross," said Brenda. John tried making sense out of Brenda's favourite song, he then fixed his gaze on Brenda and asked her if actually the best things in life are free, and if that's always the case.

"Sometimes you just can't place a price on things of value, some things are worth more than silver, gold, diamond, rubies and sapphiress, name it," she whispered.

"Err, you're right," he said with a nod. "The best things in life are free," they both echoed.

After about two hours in John's apartment watching the movie '17 Again', Brenda stood up.

"I think it's time to go, I've got some tidying up to do," said Brenda. "Er.., so soon," John asked.

Brenda didn't hesitate to remind John her visit wasn't planned, she made him understand they serendipitously crossed each other's path for the second time, and she decided to know where he stays so he doesn't disappear again. Brenda then burst into laughter and smiled rolling her eyeballs at him.

"I can't help but see you before the weekend, what about lunch on Tuesday?" he asked, caressing her fingers and looking into her eyes. "How? I'll be in the office then," she said. "But you do go for lunch break, right? We need to work something out," John said, anxiously.

"Yeah, I do go for lunch, what's your pleasure?" asked Brenda. John then pleaded with Brenda to please try and make out time for him by noon on Tuesday.

"Wait a minute, John, are you asking me out, on a date?" Brenda asked. "Yeah, maybe, officially," John replied.

Brenda was a bit wary about the timing for her date with John and suggested that hanging out is best in the evening, after the day's work. "This isn't a real date, it's just some kind of catching up, and the real date will come up over the weekend," John said, with excitement.

"Ok, whatever," she said, with a shrugging gesture yet remained upbeat about the whole thing. The conversation continued as she walks into John's bathroom to freshen up before leaving.

"What about we meet up for lunch, by taking our lunch break the same time?" asked John.

She walks out of the bathroom picks up her bag and makes her way to the door and John follows her from behind as they continued their conversation in the elevator.

"Ok, we'll talk about that later today, or maybe tomorrow, and agree on a time," said Brenda, as he walked her to the car park where her car was parked.

"I need to give you my contact card, so you don't give me new excuses," Brenda said, as she stretched out her hand for John's phone number. Funnily, John was quick to tell Brenda there won't be any excuse now that his sight is fixed on her and frankly, he made it clear to her he'll be thinking of her all day.

She took John's phone number from him and saved her number in his phone, and then dialled hers from John's phone. "We now have each other's number, so we'll talk later," said Brenda, and she looked at John with some love and then gave him a big kiss on the cheek and a big hug, before stepping into her car.

"See you around, John," she said.

"Cheers, that's lovely," John said, as he waves her goodbye, she reversed her car, waved one final goodbye, and drove off.

Later that evening, John dialled Brenda's number, the moment she picked the call and said, "oh John," John's heart skipped. "Hi,"

John said with a smile on his end of the phone. "Ooh John, it's a good thing you called," said Brenda. I just want to thank you for coming around today," John said. "My pleasure," she replied. "What about Tuesday?" John asked. "What about it? We've got that covered, I guess," Brenda said, in a soft spoken tone.

John urged her they need to meet up for lunch, and that he can't wait to see her again, and apologised for his anxiety as his heart beats faster and his breath became heavier on the phone, but Brenda smiled as she perceives John's blood rush. John on the other hand, isn't perturbed about his vulnerability being in full glare, because he's quite convinced that with Brenda he's in a safe hand. "We agreed to take things slow, didn't we?" she asked. "Yeah, yeah, said John, I can see my emotions unravelling before my eyes, and I just can't help it," he said.

"Ok, Tuesday 1.30pm is the time, let's make it a date," she said, and smiled. "That'll be fantastic," said John. Brenda offered to take John to a special spot for their lunch date, and unsurprisingly, John is up for whatever spot Brenda picks, what matters most to him is that she's in attendance. He jokingly told her he's assured that her special spot is going to be as perfect as she looks.

"You'll pick me up from my office, so we can drive down in your car, as a couple," she said smiling.

When Tuesday came, John drove to Brenda's office and they both went for a lunch date, John was all smiles as he was smitten with Brenda.

They chatted, giggled, and laughed all through as if they've been friends forever.

After lunch on Tuesday, John drove Brenda back to her office. She gave him a big hug and a kiss on the cheek, he then returned to his car and waved goodbye as he reversed his car and returned to his office. Though, Celine looked around for John at the usual cafe where colleagues including John usually go for lunch, and sadly, she couldn't find him.

The moment John stepped into the office Celine fixed her gaze on him. "Where have you been, John?" she asked. "Err, I went for lunch," John replied in a hesitant manner. "Where, John? She asked, I looked around for you at the cafe but couldn't find you," said Celine.

He quickly told her he went somewhere else for lunch, at least for a change. Funnily, Celine stood up and drew closer to him as they had their conversation.

"What fragrance is that?" she asked in a meddling manner "and that isn't your perfume," said Celine. Interestingly, John knew Celine was right but he has to make the whole thing seem like nothing. "What perfume are you talking about?" He asked in his usual rhetorical fashion. Convinced that the fragrance on John is feminine, Celine unwittingly prodded John with further questions. "Were you with a lady? You may've been hugged by a lady, or were you frolicking with one?" she asked, in a desperate tone as her voice cracks. "How do you know?" John asked. "So it's true. Who's she, John?" she asked.

John is now trying as best as could to wriggle himself out of Celine's scrutiny, he then walked away from Celine and sat at his desk. Interestingly, Philip suddenly cuts into the conversation in support of Celine's observation. "John, you're actually wearing a lady's fragrance, and your disposition speaks volumes," Philip said.

"Who's she, John? Is she a client or your girlfriend?" Celine asked, laughing but subtly expressing a deep feeling of disappointment. Philip was quite clueless about Celine's romantic attraction towards John, he considers Celine's interest in John to be nothing more but mere friendship between work colleagues.

"If that's from your girlfriend, then it's worth celebrating. I'm happy for you, John," said Philip.

Days later, at about 7pm, while John was seated on the sofa watching the TV, Maggie called John's phone.

"Hello Mum," John said. "Hello John and how're you?" Maggie asked in her usual fashion.

"I'm fine, Mum," John responds, and "I suppose, your next question will be...," said John. "Maggie cuts in, where are you, John?" she asked. "I'm at home, and I guess, that's what you want hear," John said and smiled.

"I'm glad to hear you're at home, and you know you're used to staying late at work, so don't fault me," she said in a softly spoken manner. For all it's worth, sitting on the fence isn't Maggie's strong suit. It's arguably obvious that Maggie isn't just implying that John should just stay all by himself at home, she wants him to socialise, and not replace one form of doldrums with another.

"That was before, mum," John said. How's Brenda? Asked Maggie. "She's fine," said John. Maggie asked John to put Brenda on the phone, so she can speak with her. She's keen to see John do things differently, and she wanted to meet Brenda but firstly needed to hear from the soft-spoken gentle lady John told her about. "She isn't here, maybe some other time," said John.

"When are you bringing her over? I'll like to meet her," Maggie insists.

"I'll, Mum. I just need a perfect time," John said, in a reassuring voice.

Maggie wants more and she's willing to facilitate John's relationship with Brenda, and told John there's never a perfect time. She pressed on John to make out time to bring Brenda over if she's is such a nice lady as he has said, and humorously, left a casual word of caution for John as she warned him not to mess things up with Brenda by kicking this into the long grass.

No worries, Mum, I'll make time and let you know when it'll be," he said and smiled. John promised to tell Brenda about Maggie's request, but assured his mum there isn't any need to be worried about him. It was Saturday, and Philip gave John a call reminding him of the usual Saturday evening drinks at the pub. Obviously, John has plans to visit Brenda in her apartment and he's in no mood to skip this dream visit for anything in the world.

"Mate, you left the office early yesterday, I said I would check on you," said Philip.

"Yeah, I'm good, but I've a need to attend to some matter of concern," said John.

"What about 5pm? Celine will be there?" Philip asked.

"Sorry mate, I won't make it, I've got other plans," He said. "Why, John?" Philip queried further. "I've an appointment for 6pm," said John.

Funnily, Philip was disappointed that John wouldn't be joining them for the Saturday evening happy hour drinks as he told him there won't be much fun without him. "Sorry mate, I owe you this one, and I'll make it up to you," John assured.

Brenda prepared a nice dish awaiting John's arrival. It was steak, potatoes, and vegetables with onion gravy. She prepared a chocolate pudding for desert and made sure John's choice of red wine was available.

It was 6.pm and John was already at the entrance of Brenda's apartment complex, he dialled her apartment number and Brenda allowed him up, he stepped out of the elevator in the twelfth floor and walked through the corridor of the floor towards Brenda's apartment and Brenda was at the door to receive him. "Hi," he said, as she hugged him and gave him a kiss on the cheek. "Hi, and welcome to my house," she replied.

Brenda handed John a glass of red wine and showed him to the dining area, they both walked in locked step to the dining table.

"Hmm, I feel so important, and also, so loved," John said, with a feeling of excitement. "You must be joking?" Brenda said, but as she began opening the dishes the aroma escaped and enveloped the dining area.

"Oh, nice aroma, I thought your beauty would overshadow your culinary skills, but I was wrong," John said, jokingly. They started with the starter as they gradually enjoyed savouring the moment, and moments after having the starters Brenda brought the main course.

It didn't take long before she began dishing out the food onto the plate, and interestingly, John took the first scoop and enjoyed the taste and then nodded his head in affirmation of the taste of the food, Brenda looked on and laughed. They engaged in long conversation as they ate their meals and laughed.

Moments after their meal, "I had recommended you for the next master chef award," said John.

"Hmm, stop being cheeky, did you really enjoy my cooking?" She asked.

"Hmm, I scored you a plus plus plus because the food was lovely and tastes nice, and interestingly, you're a bundle of surprises." John said, as she burst into laughter.

"Wait a minute," said Brenda. She then stood up and picked up her remote and then turned up the volume of the music as she switched the song to the music of Luther Vandross titled "So Amazing".

John expressed surprise the moment the music of Luther Vandross "so Amazing" began playing, because he didn't remember telling Brenda this is one of his favourite tracks. "How did you know?" asked John.

"Know what? I don't seem to be following," said Brenda. She then stretched out her hand in a gesture inviting John to dance with her.

"How do you know I love this song?" John asked again.

"Oh, this song? You told me about it," Brenda said, pulling John up from his seat as he hesitated.

"I did?" John asked, I never remembered.

"Come and dance with me, John," she insisted as she pulls him up. John was quite hesitant and tried excusing himself as he told Brenda they just finished eating a sumptuous meal, and he feels a bit lazy. He however sluggishly got up from his seat and joined Brenda on the dance floor. He passed his hands around her waist and nibbled into her ears and said he loves her to bits.

"It doesn't matter, come on, and dance with me," Brenda said, as she passed her hands around John's shoulder.

Though, not long, "So amazing" was over, and as they attempt to dance to the next song, Brenda protested. "No, hold me like this, and place this hand on my waist," she said as they danced to the next music of Elvis Presley, "Gotta Lotta Living To Do," followed by the music of Sonia Spence, "Jet Plane".

John began to dance in excitement, and he enjoyed every bit of the moment. He was quite at the tempo of his emotions, and he then pulled her to himself.

"You smell so good," He said, showing signs of a man in cloud nine. Brenda burst into laughter.

"Really, and I suppose you aren't smitten by my outfit?" Brenda asked as she smiled.

"I'm already head over heels in love with you. I suppose, you see what you're doing to me?" He said, as he winked his eye.

"I'm beginning to blush, John," She said, and then she lays her head on his shoulder, as they dance.

John finds himself smiling all along, and began whispering into Brenda's ear.

"Oh my God, Brenda, I just realised you're going to steal my heart without me knowing it. I'm very taken by your choice of songs, right atmosphere, and a pretty lady by my side, what else can a man ask for?" he whispered.

"I'm not stealing your heart, you'll hand it to me yourself, let's just take things slowly." Brenda said, as she burst into laughter.

"Thank you for making my weekend count for something, I can't ask for more after receiving an ecstatic reception," John said.

After an hour of dancing, and enjoying each other's company, it's now time for John to return to his place. Brenda walked him to the car park where they said bye to each other, and Brenda gave John a kiss on his cheek, then waved him good night and John returned home. The moment John entered his car and drove off, he called Brenda's phone and they continued their conversation until John got to his place. They continued their conversation until late before saying good night to each other.

John and Brenda's relationship blossomed in the weeks following as they spent more time together, enjoying each other's company. Sadly, John's relationship with his colleagues is beginning to suffer, and the usual time out with Philip and Celine to enjoy the happy hours together seems to have taken the hit.

Weeks later, Philip wants to know why John has stopped joining them for drinks on Saturday evenings and even the occasional weekday's time out. John's colleagues noticed the sudden change in his routine lately, and even though he hasn't hinted them of his new found love, they seem convinced that there's something behind the change in his routine. While John was in the office flipping through the pages of documents in the file opened before him, Philip drew close to him.

"John, what's going on?" Philip asked. "What? I don't understand what you mean," replied John as he flips through the content of the files and turning to Philip.

"I mean, the usual Saturday evenings we spend together for drinks," Philip explained. "Yeah, what about it?" John asked.

"You don't show up anymore, and I'm used to enjoying your company," said Philip. John was hesitant but it now dawned on him that his friendship with his colleagues is under threat, and he'd to apply some wisdom in dealing with the situation. John stopped what he's doing as he told Philip it's nothing actually, and he equally missed their hanging out as well, but his schedules are currently tight. John really didn't want to let out too much, he decided to put a sock in it until he's sure his relationship with Brenda is rock-solid and won't say more about his escapades. Interestingly, Celine cuts into the conversation to add her voice to the mix.

"I don't know what happened to my John, he came back from his lunch break the other day wearing feminine cologne," said Celine. Lesley became jocular and said maybe John is in love but Celine on the other hand insisted, saying that can't be true because she would be the first to know if John is in love.

"My hunch tells me there's something about John's new disposition, and remember, you said he came back from lunch wearing feminine cologne," Lesley said. But Celine can't accept any slight indication that John has found a woman different from her for himself.

"I suppose, John met an old acquaintance who gave him an innocent hug that meant nothing, that's all," Celine retorted. Lesley looked on and smiled but didn't stop short to prove her point as she laid bare the new features associated with the new John. She told Celine that John giggles, smiles and laughs more than he's used to which are indication he's in love, she then looked at John and smiled. Sensing that Lesley's assertions might be right, and attempting to curtail her frustrations Celine continue banging the same drum, as she insists, she disagrees with Lesley, and made it emphatically clear to all in the room that John can only be in love with one person, and that's her. Arguably, the social interplay between John and Celine isn't all pink and flurry, it's somewhat complicated and hard to decipher, this sort of leave colleagues clueless about what it is between this two.

With his eyes still fixed on the files on his desk, John raised his head to make eye contact with his colleagues and retorted, "guys I'm still in the room." Philip cuts into the conversation. "Sorry, John, the ladies changed the theme of our conversation from Saturday night out, to your personal stuff."

"I understand, but there isn't anything to know, I just chose to do things differently, but everything will soon fall back into place," John insists. Interestingly, Philip didn't really want to join issues but seem to see some sense in what the ladies have said.

"Err, mate, but if you're actually in love, spare us the mystery, and give us the privilege of meeting her," said Philip.

In one of the lunch breaks, while John's was still playing hide and seek with his colleagues. Celine decided to go on a self-appointed investigative mission in a bid to unravel the mystery behind the fragrance that follows John whenever he returns from his lunch break.

She originally intended to tail John's car but duty calls in the office made her miss the opportunity for that. She then decided to follow her hunch as she traced John to the possible place she guessed holds the secret of his mystery, "the big fish garden."

Unfortunately, it rained cats and dogs that morning, and funnily, the rain didn't deter Celine from daring to uncover what mystery was wrapped up John's sleeve. As expected, after a heavy rainfall, the grass carpet of the garden was quite soaked with water and it was quite squishy as she walked up and about trying to seek John out from his hiding, but she didn't find him. This mission was a big failure. She then returned to the office and pretended such investigation never happened because she never mentioned it to John, and neither did she mention it to anyone.

By Thursday evening, John took Brenda out for dinner at the Hilton Docklands Riverside in London. After dinner they drove straight to John's house where she's meant to pass the night.

"This outing was fun," she said, as they entered John's apartment. John on the other hand muttered, saying he thinks they should do this again, very soon. He then stopped as though he just realised something he forgot.

"Just wait a minute," John said as he rushed for the remote and quickly played a song titled "I Believe in You and Me" by Whitney Houston. "Let's dance some more, just us alone this time, in our own space," he said with a smile. Brenda seems to relish the idea of them alone in their own space.

They danced, giggled, and laughed as they enjoyed each other's warmth and company for a while before Brenda felt it's time to retire but decided to take her shower before going to bed. While Brenda was in the Bath, the night couldn't get weirder until John offered to join her. "Can I join you in the bath?" He asked.

"What! Join me? I don't think so," She protested. Funnily, they haven't taken their romance this far, and this is quite far from what Brenda understand as taking things slow. "Why? John asked, I've always dreamt of being in the bath with a classy, pretty woman," he said. Sadly, that's a no no for Brenda. "John, not now, I'm shy," said Brenda.

"You don't have to be shy, because I'm coming in with a glass of red wine for you and with my eyes shut," John said in a reassuring tone.

"Ok then, come in but make sure your eyes are closed, and walk straight into the bath, but don't forget my glass of wine," she said.

"Ok, as it pleases Your Majesty," he said, as he walked into the bath, and then opened his eyes. Brenda tried keeping the ambience friendly.

"Welcome to my world, and is this a dream come true for you? I supposed you peeped even when you promised to keep your eyes shut?" she asked, jokingly.

"Yeah, just a bit of peeping, but never mind, I didn't see anything," John said, as he tried to assure Brenda.

"Never mind, just have as much fun as you want, and after all, we've been friends forever, right?" asked Brenda. John couldn't help himself as he looked straight into Brenda's eyes and told her she's an epitome of happy memories, she really doesn't know how he feels right now. She felt quite shy and turned her back at John, but after a while Brenda turned to John, and asked.

"How do you feel, then?" she asked.

"This isn't just cloud nine, I just can't explain the feeling, and I can't believe this is really happening," John continued to blab in his vulnerable and emotionally entangled state. Interestingly, she will stop at nothing until John's emotion gets the best of him.

"You mean, cloud nine? Cloud nine is a general state of feeling, I won't stop at cloud nine, I start from cloud nine, and just let me know, when your emotion goes beyond cloud nine," she advised.

"Ok, paradise, call it anything. Having a pretty classy lady like you with me in a bath is a bash, and means more than you think to me," said John.

Brenda needed to stop John from blabbing further, she then assured him that if this means so much to him, then they will have to do this again. "Oh, I look forward to more of this," John said, laughing.

After taking their bath, John carried Brenda to the bedroom, "oh I like this, but gently," she cautioned.

"Oh, ok, but the timing is perfect, the atmosphere is perfect, the night is perfect, and with the perfect person" John said, and then asked Brenda, "what do you think?"

"Then let's make the best of it," she said, as they spent all night in each other's arms, and as early as 6.am the next morning John dropped Brenda off at her place so she could prepare for work.

John has a nice physique, just that his work seem to have sucked him in, and being someone disposed towards classy ladies he doesn't seem to be doing enough to make himself look more than the regular guy.

With Brenda now in the scene, there's now a sudden need for John to go the extra mile of upgrading his outfits to something more elegant and posh in a manner that matches' Brenda's posh status. He spent some of his time on some trendy magazines, borrowing tips that will help him look a bit posh. As the days and weeks passed by, John had no idea he's changed in a manner of outfits and social disposition, the tips from the magazines seem to have been quite helpful to help John rise to the occasion.

Weeks later, in her usual fashion, Brenda was to travel to Paris for the fashion week, but just realised the event is ongoing and will be rounding up by weekend and felt the need to be in the company of her newly found love. It was Thursday, and Brenda called John on his mobile to inform him of her intention to travel to Paris.

The moment John picked up his phone, "hey baby, speak to me," said John.

"I just realised I should be in Paris this weekend," she said. John expressed surprise but didn't hesitate to ask.

"To do what in Paris?" She laughed because this information is coming just too sudden. "This knee jerk reaction is expected, but I need to attend the walk on the runway," she said. "Walk on the runway, how do you mean?" John asked, expressing a feeling of disappoint, since he already had plans of spending his weekend with Brenda.

She made John understand that this week is the last week of the Paris Fashion Week, and it'll be rounding off by the weekend.

Being the regular guy he is, John asked, "I know you're a fashion conscious person but what has Paris fashion week got to do with you?"

She quickly told John she's attending the walk on the runway, and this is what she does yearly to keep up with her fashion. John seems not to be following as he's trying so hard to get his head around why the person he's meant to spend the weekend with should be heading to Paris.

"I don't seem to get you, I suppose, the walk on the runway, is for artists, fashion designers, and possibly, for celebrities?" He asked.

"No, it's for every fashion-conscious person who believes in fashion, and you know I'm fashion-conscious," she said, in a whisper as she tries to convince him.

"Does it mean I'll be spending the weekend alone?" John protested.

"No, I mean you should come with me to Paris," Brenda offered. John's ingenuity gets the best of him, as he now thought of using one stone to kill two birds and proposed they watch the Paris fashion week on TV, and forget about travelling to Paris.

"I need to be there in person, this trip is imperative because it'll help me decide what designer to go for," Brenda said, as she continues to try persuading John via the phone. Funnily, while John was on the phone with Brenda, Celine walked to Lesley's desk, which was next to John's, and an attempt to keep things under wraps, John conceded and said. "Ok, you win."

"Oh my God! This is sweet, I'll come over to your house tonight so we can book our flight and make arrangements," she said, in excitement.

"Ok then, see you later," John said, but his attempt to bring the conversation to a quick end because of Celine's presence wasn't possible since Brenda still had something to say.

"Before you drop the phone, I think it'll be better we leave tomorrow evening," Brenda said. John stood up, pretending to be in search of a document, then walked away from his desk where Celine was and moved to the other end of the office and opened a filing cabinet while he continued his conversation with Brenda. "Why tomorrow? That'll be Friday," said John.

"Spending Friday night together in a new environment will be a plus for us, I suppose. What do you think?" Brenda asked. John concurred, and by close of work they met at John's place to conclude arrangements.

That night John and Brenda booked a British Airways flight, for Friday night, and by Friday night they landed at Charles De Gaulle airport, and checked into the hotel. They spent Friday in each other's arms, and on Saturday morning they left for the show, and the moment they walked into the venue, Brenda noticed her preferred sitting position is vacant, she held John by the hand as they made their way to Brenda's preferred sitting position. Though, John is a regular guy and this whole run-way thing is new to him, but he seemed to love the atmosphere, enjoying being a part of it.

"Oh babe, it's a good thing I'm a witness to this show," John said, expressing a feeling of excitement.

"This is all new to you, and I know you've not been here before from the way you sounded when I told you about it," said Brenda. John held her hand as he confirmed to her he never expected it would be this much fun.

"Good to hear you love the experience," she said and leaned on John's shoulder.

"I hesitated at first but this whole trip has been fun all the way and this trip is an eye-opener," said John.

"An eye opener, I suppose? Now you know, the walk on the runway isn't only for celebrities," Brenda said, as they watched the show. Interestingly, a moment of magical silence occurred between them, and realising they've been unusually silent, John turned to Brenda and asked.

"What just happened? I mean the sudden silence," said John.

"Maybe an angel just passed through our corner, I guess," Brenda said jocularly. John smiled and said the sudden silence was quite eerie and suggested they continue talking to stop that eerie silence from returning.

By the close of the day which concluded the fashion week, John and Brenda moved from one end of the venue to another, and at some point John turned to her and asked if she has made up her mind on any of the designers. "Err.., I'm still making up my mind but I've spotted something nice to enhance my looks," she replied.

The pair concluded their experience on an interesting note, and by the close of the day, they headed for their hotel room and later proceeded to the airport.

As they set off to board their return flight to London, John looked at Brenda keenly and said, "I hope I'll not lose you, because everything about you is classy," he said. But Brenda seems to have a prepared response for John, as she tried to assuage his worries.

"Don't tell me John Watson is worried about losing his woman," she replied and they both burst into laughter and the hysteria took over.

CHAPTER
THREE

The Competition

John's lifestyle changed dramatically, his social life improved, and he became more engaging in conversation. Consequently, the lifestyle of staying behind in the office after his colleagues at the law firm have closed for the day stopped.

On one of his outings with Brenda in the O2 Arena, where they both went to watch Tina Turner perform live, the pair decided to have some time to themselves before Tina Turner came on stage.

John then ordered red wine for himself and Brenda, as they both enjoyed each other's company chatting away and laughing, sipping from their glasses of wine. One of the English Premier League stars, who also came to watch Tina Turner perform walked past John and Brenda, then stopped suddenly and walked back to Brenda.

Hello, sweet lady, he said. Brenda noticed the person in front of him and exclaimed.

"Oh, you're William Brent, the football star, I suppose! Nice to meet you," she said," she then extends her hand for a handshake.

"Yeah, you caught my attention and I can't help it but stop for a chat," he said.

"Oh, that's nice of you, thank you," said Brenda. Sadly, William continues to dawdle and he isn't ready to be on his way that soon, at least, not without making his move on Brenda.

"Look around, you're the prettiest thing in this entire arena," said William.

"You must be joking," she said, as she burst into laughter. Interestingly, William needs to keep the conversation going but finds it fitting to begin with flattery before straying into other areas to keep the conversation up.

"What do you think about tonight? I mean the artist," William asked.

"Ooh my god, I love it. I'd love to hear that "What's Love Got to Do" song once more," Brenda said, with a gesture of some dance moves. William was taken over by Brenda's charm and couldn't leave without making a pass at her, yet John is now uncomfortable and he's beginning to find William to be a distraction, and in John's heart 'three is a crowd.

"Please, can I just have a word with you?" He said, in a soft tone. Sadly, Brenda isn't up for that. "Sorry, that won't be possible, as you can see, I'm with someone," said Brenda.

"Why? I just need a few minutes with you," he pressed. The friendly atmosphere is fast fading away, and William is no longer welcome.

"You ask me, why? I won't dignify your question with a response," she retorted, with a frown. John fixed his gaze at William with disgust as he tried to control his outrage.

"I like you, I truly like you." William said. "You're beginning to bore me, William, and that's rude," said Brenda. Sadly, John is now feeling so irritated and infuriated, he then exploded in anger. "Whatever you say your name is, please excuse us. Don't make me do something stupid," said John. "Ok, ok, you guys are taking this the wrong way," William retorted, and then walks away.

"Please can I just have a word with you?" He said, in a soft tone. Sadly, Brenda isn't up for that.

"Sorry, that won't be possible, as you can see, I'm with someone," said Brenda.

"Why? I just need a few minutes with you," he pressed. The friendly atmosphere is fast fading away, and William is no longer welcome.

"You ask me, why? I won't dignify your question with a response," she retorted, with a frown. John fixed his gaze at William with disgust as he tried to control his outrage.

"I like you, I truly like you." William said. You're beginning to bore me, William, and that's rude," said Brenda. Sadly, John is now feeling so irritated and infuriated, he then exploded in anger. "Whatever you say your name is, please excuse us. Don't make me do something stupid," said John. "Ok, ok, you guys are taking this the wrong way," William said, and walks away.

Weeks later, Brenda ran into Michael, her high school flame, who actually was her first love. Michael is as quintessential as Brenda, which is one feature they both share in common. Michael came to Brenda's office to discuss available properties to rent or buy, and David, Brenda's work colleague was attending to him when Brenda walked into the office, and Michael's attention shifted immediately in surprise.

"Excuse me, you must be Brenda!" Michael exclaimed. Brenda turned around to see who it was.

"What! Michael, that's you, I suppose?" asked Brenda.

Michael stood up and rushed to Brenda, and without hesitation, they hugged each other tightly. "What a miracle!" He exclaimed.

"What are you doing in my office?" she asked in excitement.

"I came to checkout some properties, do you work here?" he replied.

"Yeah, I work here, what about you?" she queried further. He told her he just moved in from Canada last week because his firm is opening a new branch here in London. They chatted for a while, for a brief catching up and while still holding Brenda by the hand.

"You left for Canada without saying goodbye, Michael," Brenda said, in a soft-spoken tone, expressing disappointment.

"My parents moved, and I didn't have a choice, and meanwhile I was just a teenager but I take the blame for everything," said Michael. Brenda doesn't seem to be buying Michel's excuses as she narrated the pain of trying so hard to reach him but all efforts failed. Michael on the other hand tried making light of the situation, by trying to be a bit romantically cheeky with Brenda to see if there's a possibility of a reconnection.

"Looking at how fashion conscious you were back in the day, I expect that by now you have moved from C cup to triple D," said Michael as he whispering into her ear.

"Shush! Don't be a spoilt man," Brenda cautioned with a smile.

"Sorry, that's me being spoilt," he jokingly said.

Michael continued to plead with Brenda as he told her, what happened was a temporary lapse of judgement on his part, and he's still paying the price for losing her. It's been sixteen years since they last saw each other, and they were inseparable teens until Michael's parents moved to Canada.

"You were moving to Canada with your parents and never cared to talk about it with your girlfriend and you called that a temporary lapse of judgement, seriously? Gosh, don't give me that crap," Brenda retorted.

"That's why I'm yet to get married," said Michael, looking straight into Brenda's blue eyes.

"Wow! Then what are you waiting for?" she asked.

"Someone like you," He said.

"You'll tell me all about that later, after you're through with David," she said, as she noticed a client is waiting to be attended to.

"Give me your card, and I'll check on you," he said. Interestingly, while Michael was still in a conversation with Brenda, David called out to him.

"Michael, come on, let's conclude on this," said David. He enthusiastically without hesitation told David he will join him in a minute, yet didn't hesitate to let him know Brenda was his classmate in high school. Interestingly, Michael would stop at nothing in pulling all the stops to get back what he lost sixteen years ago, and didn't stop short of letting David know Brenda was his first love.

"Ok, should I give you time to catch up with Brenda and we do this some other time, what's your pleasure?" asked David.

"Err, there's so much to talk about and our catching up will take forever, let's do this, David," said Michael. "Go, go, he doesn't like to be kept waiting," said Brenda. "Who?" Michael asked. "David of course, we'll do a proper catching up later," said Brenda.

Going for lunch together has been the norm since John invited Brenda for a lunch date when their relationship started. They usually meet up at their favourite spot but on this occasion, Brenda took her car to the mechanic workshop and then took the bus to meet up with John in the office so they could go for lunch together. Although, this is the first time Brenda is checking up on John in his place of work. Over the past few months John's colleagues at the law firm became aware that he's in a relationship. This explains the reason why he no longer stays back in the office beyond the normal closing time. He has also stopped the usual going out for drinks with colleagues on Saturday evenings. He goes elsewhere for lunch outside the usual place he eats with his colleagues during their lunch break. In addition to the fact that after each lunch break there's this feminine fragrance that's usually perceived on his body.

However, John's colleagues are convinced that it's only a love affair that'll cause a dramatic change in a man's lifestyle. The questions that remain unanswered is who the lady is, and what she looks like. These and many more questions remained unanswered in the mind of John's colleagues at work as they grapple with the new John Watson that's unravelling before their eyes. They always teased him about his new love affair to see if he would open up, but he will usually laugh it away and has never budged on the details.

That afternoon, as soon as Brenda stepped into the law firm dressed in her Jacquard skirt suit, Philip welcomed her and mistook her for a client. John was with Tom Bradley in his office while Celine and Lesley were having a conversation about a client's case when Brenda walked in.

"Hello, good afternoon," said Philip. "Hi," she said, with a smile. "How can we help you today?" asked Philip. "Err, yeah, I've come to see John," Brenda replied.

Brenda's statement drew Celine's attention. Celine's focus shifted immediately towards Brenda, and she immediately noticed the fragrance Brenda was wearing was exactly the same as the one that she perceives on John whenever he returns from lunch. Celine stopped her conversation with Lesley abruptly as she spent the next few seconds assessing Brenda, who pretended not to have noticed the obvious censure from Celine.

The confusion with Celine was that she never expected John's woman to be this pretty and classy.

"Hmm, ok, you're welcome, please have a seat," Philip said, as he shows her where to sit.

"Thank you," Brenda said, with a smile that displayed her dimples visibly. "Is he expecting you?" Philip asked,

"Yeah," Brenda replied.

"Ok, he'll join you in a minute," Philip said. Though, charmed by Brenda's look, Philip didn't realise that Brenda is John's woman. Unsurprisingly, while Brenda remained seated and waiting for John, Celine pretended to focus on her work but was obviously distracted from her work as so many questions raced through her mind, concerning Brenda's personality.

Moments later, John spotted Brenda as he stepped out of Tom Bradley's office and walked up to her. "Hi, you seem very busy," said Brenda. "Yeah, but not busy enough for my office to grace your presence," He said, enthusiastically, as he held her hand. Brenda stood up.

"Shall we?" she asked.

"Yeah, but wait a minute," John said, as he held her by the hand to the amazement of his female work colleagues. While still holding her hand, "let me introduce you to my colleagues," John said and walked to Philip whose focus was on Brenda at a time before being distracted by work.

"This is Brenda," John said. "I've met her already," Philip replied, but still trying to figure out the reason behind the formal introduction.

"Hi, Brenda," Philip said. Brenda responded with a "hi" and smiled. Funnily, it didn't take long for Philip to piece one and one together as he now makes sense of who's before him.

"John, is there something you aren't telling me?" asked Philip.

"I've just told you everything," said John. Realising this is John's new flame.

"Oh, my bad," Philip said. "Ok, now I get it, and I must confess you're much prettier than I expected," said Philip. Unsurprisingly, Philip stood up and gave Brenda a hug, and welcomed her formally, but Celine who's already anxious to hear what John has to say unwittingly cuts in from her sedentary position and exclaimed,

"I knew it, John! She is your girlfriend."

"You've got a good taste, John. Your waiting was not in vain, you picked a perfect one," said Philip. They all burst into laughter, Celine joined in the hysteria but John noticed Celine's frustration and her confusion even as she tried to be of good cheer. Thank you all, we'll see more each other in the coming days, and I think we've to get going," said Brenda.

"To where?" Celine asked in desperation.

"For lunch," John replied.

Philip cuts in as he turned to Brenda, "one of these days, you'll join us for drinks so we can get know each other better," he said.

"Oh, sure, that's kind of you," said Brenda.

"Go girl, and enjoy your lunch, and I suppose the spot is exotic," Celine said, in a whisper.

It's quite obvious that Brenda's return is unwittingly emancipatory for John, at least from Celine's clutches.

The moment John and Brenda stepped out of his office, Brenda's assessment became the theme of the conversation within the office. Philip's assessment of Brenda was that there's a lady in every girl but sadly, not every woman is a lady. He proceeded to conclude that Brenda on the other hand radiates the features of a lady even from afar. She seems to radiate class, which interestingly, adds colour to her beauty gifted to her by nature.

Minutes later, John drove off as they left for lunch, and funnily, while in the car Brenda became momentarily silent, as she could not get head around Celine's disposition towards her even when Celine smiled and laughed all through. Brenda sensed Celine's laughter was a veil used to mask her rivalry with her. She sensed that even when Celine didn't say much, she has already said so much by her silence. Unsurprisingly, she suddenly muttered "who is Celine to you?" Brenda asked curiously.

"How do you mean? She's just a colleague like every other person you saw in the office," John retorted.

"She seemed to be nice, but I know that look when I see it," said Brenda. John knew he needed to nip this in the bud quickly, because this could dramatically morph into something else and get dirty at his own peril. He didn't expect this drama surfacing so quickly, and didn't really like the direction of Brenda's new line of conversation, after all, they've just briefly met each other for the first time.

"What look, and what are you talking about?" John retorted.

"The look you give to a rival, I know that look even amidst smiles and giggles," she said.

John isn't one taken to greed and will never acquiesce making the attempt of riding two horses at once. All he could do was urge Brenda not to waste her time searching for something that doesn't exist, and insists Celine is just a female colleague like any other female. Brenda went straight to hit the nail on the head as she quickly pointed out to John, that he may not be interested in

Celine but she's certainly into him. John knew Brenda was right in her assertions about Celine, but felt the best way to deal with Brenda's concerns is to trivialise her perception of Celine.

"Let's not exaggerate her disposition towards you, Celine has a good heart, just like you," John said, in a bid to reassure Brenda that there isn't any rivalry between her and Celine.

"I'm only telling the tale as it is by unwittingly stating the obvious and I'm not jealous," she said, dismissively. "You already know that your beauty and style conquers rivalry," he said, and burst into laughter. Brenda joined him in the laughter and while the laughter lasted a while, Brenda was still keen to state her position on this matter.

John then looked away, yet reminded Brenda that keeping a list of pretty nasty stuff in her head is in contrast to her beauty.

Despite grappling to stay composed while thinking of a way of keeping this newly found rival constrained. She had to avoid every form of indulgence as well as making further barbs and digs at John.

"The most important thing in this whole conversation is where your interest lies," she whispered, and said nothing more about her perceived rivalry with Celine.

A few days later, Michael called Brenda and requested her address, and then decided to check on her at about 7pm, after the day's work. On his way to Brenda's house, he bought a bottle of red wine and some pink roses which he knew, used to be her favourite.

"Hello Brenda," Michael said, immediately he stepped into Brenda's apartment. He then handed her the flowers and the bottle of red wine, as he entered her apartment.

"Oh my God, you still remember my favourite flowers, and colour," she exclaimed.

"I haven't forgotten you, and I can't forget your favourites," Michael said, in a soft and romantic tone.

"Ooh that's nice, Michael, You're welcome to my house," Brenda said, as she tried to make Michael feel comfortable.

Michael adjusted himself on Brenda's Velvet's sofa to enable him make proper eye contact with Brenda while he attempts to win her back to himself.

"Coming into contact with you again is an answer to my prayers," Michael confessed. "What do you mean by that, and what prayer was answered?" she asked, as she hands him a glass of red wine, with some peanuts in a saucer.

"You and me, coming back together is a prayer answered, I've missed you so much," he expressed. Brenda wasn't particularly impressed as he accused Michael of sounding as if he owns her, particularly because he never even bothered to ask if she's in a relationship, but went on as if he's in some kind of conquest.

"Are you?" Michael asked. Michael is now looking exasperated and Brenda had to calm things down by letting Michael understand there's isn't any need for this euphemius look. She then pleaded with Michael to spare her these homilies, because she's too busy to listen to his fibs. Michael doesn't seem to want to give up easily as he pressed further, telling Brenda if he has a dozen life times, he'd spend all of it with her.

"How can you just show up after sixteen years, and expect that I'll still be available for you?" she said. Brenda's comment is an expression of anger resulting from her disappointing past with Michael.

"I know you aren't married, and I equally know, we're meant for each other," Michael presses further.

"I'm in a relationship, his name is John," said Brenda. Michael's hope of having Brenda back seemed to be on the wire, but he isn't giving up yet as he now resorted to emotional appeal. "Oh my God, Brenda. I don't want to lose you again," he pleaded.

"Stop this, Michael. Don't make this reunion more difficult for the both of us," Brenda said. She then looks away from Michael as her emotion was being put on trial because she truly loved Michael but that's over, now. Michael suddenly realised he's now sounding like a big phony, and decided to change tack. This guy is unassuming, he's now like a sponge, wiling to absorb everything and anything, including the rejection, and this time, he felt his skill of moral suasion will be handy at this point, since Brenda isn't budging, he decided to take her back to the memory lane of their romantic past. "Do you remember our first kiss?" He asked, smiling. "Yeah, under the staircase," she said.

"Do you remember our first night together?" He asked further.

"Of course, I do, it was in your dad's house, and there wasn't anyone at home," she said. Brenda quickly sensed that Michael was toying with her emotions and she thought it best to allow Michael tire himself out, as opposed to being confrontational towards him.

"Have you forgotten about those first-time experiences?" He asked and burst into laughter, as he took a sip from his glass of wine.

"No one forgets their first time, such moments are never forgotten," she replied. Michael stood up to draw closer to Brenda but returned to his seat to avoid being seen to be creepy, after all, they have been apart for sixteen years and too much water has gone under the bridge. "I want to continue with you, to preserve those memories," he said, with a look of someone begging for acceptance.

"This is empiricism, Michael. Why're you doing this?" she asked.

"You remain unperturbed despite all effort to restore what we had," he said. He then stood up again from the sofa and drew close to her, yet avoided pushing his luck too far by being polite and keeping some distance from her, to avoid muddying the water too quickly.

"Why don't we talk about something else?" she walks away from Michael and walks to her refrigerator to get a glass of water.

"I'm only assuaging your critical mind-set about me," he pressed further. "What should I do about John?" she asked. "You know what to say to him," he said, in a cautious tone, to avoid being branded heartless. Michael reappearance at this particular point in time is blast from the past that could possibly rock the boat for Brenda.

"How? You seem not to be listening. I said I'm in a relationship," she emphasised.

"Come on, Brenda, I know your favourite flower and colour better than he does," said Michael. This time he drew closer to her and attempted holding her hand. "Don't do that, don't touch me," she retorted as she pulls herself away from him. Unfortunately, Brenda's hesitation is beginning to get to Michael, and his frustration is obviously beginning to reflect in his tone.

"What do you want me to do? Should I just pretend about my feelings for you?" asked Michael. He looked straight into her eyes, expecting her to give him a positive response.

"You should love someone else I suppose, it's already 10pm, and I think you should be going," she said, pointing him to the wall clock for him to see what time it is for himself. "Err..., it has come to this, are you sending me away?" he asked, in protest.

"No, of course not and I won't do that to you, Michael. I'm not sending you away; it's late, and you can't pass the night here, and you know I've to go to work tomorrow," she said, trying to calm him with some reassuring words.

Interestingly Michael needs to earn his keep, but this time his superb move seems not to be enough to make the difference, and sadly, in the present circumstance, he thought it wise to refrain from adding fuel to this already incendiary situation.

"Thank you for your hospitality, we'll continue this conversation. Remember, I haven't given up on you," said Michael. He then adjusts his suit, with jacket clasp gesture as he prepares to leave Brenda's apartment. "Holding the conversation in abeyance won't do you any good, Michael. There's nothing there for you anymore, you need to realise that," said Brenda as she walks Michael to the door and they wished each other good night, in a polite and cordial manner.

That night, Michael spent most of the night in bed reminiscing his moments with Brenda.

Despite his obvious failings in the past, Michael was willing to go the whole hog for Brenda, even willing to walk through fire for her. Sadly, Brenda doesn't need the star tumbling down from the sky, and neither does she need Michael to prove to her that what he now feels for her is far from the school-boy infatuation of sixteen years ago.

Too much water has passed under the bridge and she's now John's woman. When you love someone, say it and show it, and if not, when the opportunity passes, its gone forever.

Michael's only regret is that he didn't carry Brenda along sixteen years ago, and his failings of the past was quite needling and everything can't be the same again.

His encounter with Brenda brought this awkward awakening that he's single, and needed a woman. He now associates being single to being lonely, and Michael now hates being stuck in the rot of loneliness. There's this sudden dawning on Michael that makes him consider loneliness as everything but benign.

His fat pay cheque, his big personality, his sociable nature and even his warm disposition doesn't mean the nights aren't lonely sometimes. He's no longer interested in a part-time lover; he now wants a woman of his own. Unfortunately, Brenda is no longer for the taking.

Celine, on her part, felt the need to up her game, to avoid John slipping away from her grasp. Interestingly, two weekends after John introduced Brenda to his colleagues at work, Celine drove to John's place without giving him any notice she was coming. It was a Saturday morning and John was at home doing his laundry. When she arrived at the apartment complex where John was living, Celine pressed the bell to John's apartment. "Hello, who is it?" he asked.

"John, it's me, Celine," she replied.

"Hmm, Celine?" John asked, expressing surprise because he wasn't expecting her. John allowed her into the apartment without any tingle of anticipation that this visit is nothing but aromantic. Unsurprisingly, immediately Celine stepped into John's apartment John didn't hesitate to express his surprise at her impromptu visit.

"It's just 9am and what are you doing in my area?" John asked curiously. "Hi John," Celine said in a soft spoken tone. "What are you doing outside this early? I wasn't expecting company" John said.

"I just came to spend some time with you, are you nervous or what?" she asked.

"Of course not, but....."

Celine interrupted while John was still speaking.

"But what, John? I was bored, and I decided to come and spend some time with a friend. Do you have issues with that?" she asked.

"Ok, you're welcome and please make yourself comfortable," John said, as he tried to calm her frayed nerves. Funnily, instead of sitting on the sofa, Celine pulled out one of the chairs in John's dining and kept it close to where John was doing his laundry and they began chatting about their domestic chores. "I've got wine, brandy, and champagne, what's your pleasure?" asked John.

"Give me brandy," she replied. John brought her a glass and hands her a bottle of Brandy to pour herself her desired measure of brandy.

"Give me your jacket," John requested. He then collects her winter jacket and hangs it for her. Celine walks to the refrigerator and opens it to see what's available that she could have for breakfast.

"What do you have for breakfast?" she asked.

"You'll give me some time to finish what I'm doing, so I can make you breakfast," John said.

"Don't worry, I'll make it myself," she offered.

"Everything is in the refrigerator, just help yourself," John said.

She made cheese on toast with bacon for herself, and supported it with a hot cup of tea, but felt the need to make something for John. "John, what do want for breakfast? I'm having cheese on toast with bacon," she asked.

"Make the same for me," John replied.

Moments later, the breakfast was ready.

"You should be ready to have your breakfast now, I suppose, because you won't enjoy it when it's cold," she said, as she set the table for breakfast. "Yeah, I'm almost done with washing up and will join you in a moment," he said.

"You know it's wrong to keep a lady waiting." Celine retorted as she takes the first bite of her cheese on toast. Understanding the fine line between reality and fantasy has nothing to do with this, because Celine knows when best to bring in her platitudes.

"Oh, you're right, I'm coming right away," he said and joins her at the table. They ate breakfast and chatted about work, the happy hours they spent together and other things they have in common, but along the line, Celine tried moving the subject of the conversation away from a general perspective to a more personal issue.

"Why didn't you join me in bed the last time I was here?" she asked.

"Nothing, I just chose to sleep on the couch that day, and that shouldn't bother you," John said, keeping a straight face.

"Well, it bothered me," she replied.

"Ok, I'm sorry, if that bothered you," he apologised to her with a brief smile.

"Ok, let's put the past behind us, at least I'm here with you today," she said, in a romantically soft tone. But John's desire to keep things civil doesn't mean allowing Celine to lure him into a romantic relationship, which never happened while he was single, and mustn't happen now that he's in a committed relationship.

"I don't understand, what do you mean you're here today?" He queried.

"Yeah," Celine said, as she got up from her seat, and started fondling John. She then continued.

"I mean... Hmm, I'm sorry I'm not in the mood for this now," said John. He then stood up and tried taking her hands off him. Oops that didn't go down well she thought to herself, and she suddenly came to the realisation that there will be many more oops moments if this stunt of hers will turn out a success, yet prefers to fight on as opposed to giving in.

"And why the trepidation?" she asked, expressing some disgust.

"I'm not wavering, Celine. You need to stop this," He said.

"Then when will you be ready for me? I need to know," she stressed. John is now a captive audience of Celine, and as far as John is concerned, Celine's flirtatious moves seem to have crossed acceptable boundaries of what's best a platonic relationship.

Celine fixed her gaze at John, expecting a response, but John isn't ready for any school boy infidelity, and he finds that any away match behind Brenda will be prickly awkward, because it might end up being a sting in the tail. John feared that this kind of stunt is a reminder of how quickly fatal attractions turns into a lethal concoction, where the mistress had to kill and cook the family bunny and all that. While working out the most polite way to dismiss Celine, the ambience between the two became awkward, as things quickly became tensed, yet John tried to remain civil, but still felt the need to assert his position on this matter, and sadly, Celine isn't having it.

"Is this why you came here today?" John asked, expressing his frustrations at her.

"What do you think about this?" She took off her top, leaving her bra on, walking around John who's already up standing at this point as he tried to ward her off. John was particularly unhappy that Celine's visit was deceptively intriguing, yet held his nerves. Celine was quite exasperated by this sudden hollow feeling that John is giving her the run around, but her knock out phrase is latently hidden in the red writing, 'you can't say you have love if you don't give it, and no one gives love enough' even though the love she's dishing out remains unsolicited. It didn't take long before she realised that this trip is nothing but setting herself up to fail and she might return home slouching, and funnily, this audacious move could have a profound impact on how she feels about John going forward.

"Celine, it's time you leave, let's not make enemies out of your visit," John said, in anger.

"Are you asking me to leave your apartment?" She asked in a depressing and disappointing tone.

"Let's not make this an awkward moment for both of us," he stressed. A sudden calm came upon her, as if there's a sudden realisation that John is offended by her actions.

"I'm sorry for putting you in an awkward position, and I get it, all you want is for us to be just friends," she said, in a calm and understanding tone.

Celine put her top back on and quietly returned to her seat. "I'm sorry about this and I don't mean to be rude, I can't think of a better friend than you," John said, as he tries to diffuse any build up of bad blood.

"Does it mean you were never in love with me?" she asked.

"Love is somehow complicated, but one thing I want you to know, is that I trust you, I like you, and I can rely on you," said John. He tried to save their friendship as he spoke to her reassuringly with his hands on her shoulders, and looking straight into her eyes.

"But, not in love with me?" she queried further as she adjusts herself on her seat.

"No, and I'm sorry if that hurts your feelings," John said.

"Is it because of Brenda?" she asked, in a low tone.

"Hmm, yeah," John replied.

"Which means, you love Brenda, much more than you love me?" she asked again.

"I'm in love with Brenda? Yes, but I like you, and you know that," John replied. "Sorry, for mistaking your likeness for me, for love. Pour some of that white wine in my glass," she said as she held up her glass for some more white wine, and then took a sip from the glass.

"Thank you," John said, in a show of appreciation. "For what?" she asked, laughing. "For still being my friend, despite all this," John said.

After calming her down, and making her not feel rejected, John played a movie which himself and Celine watched until about 1pm. When it's time for Celine to leave John's house, John walked her to the car park in the building where Celine's car was parked.

"Where did you park your car?" John asked, holding her by the hand. "Over there," said Celine. Sadly, as they took the first few steps towards Celine's car, the heavens were let loose as there was a sudden burst of rainfall, and Celine unwittingly, clinged onto John who took cover under a pillar in a bid to shed herself from the rain. Funnily, their faces were so close to each other that they could feel each other's breath as they sought cover from the rain. It was quite awkward and they both knew it. After spending a minute or two taking cover from the rain under the pillar John sensed this closeness is too close for comfort. He then suggested they return to the building, Celine nodded and they hurtled into the foyer of the building.

John then ran back to his apartment and quickly picked up the very umbrella that serendipitously connected him to Brenda and used it to provide cover for Celine.

They then walked in locked step to where Celine's car was parked, but before Celine got into her car, John held her back and said. "You're still my best friend, Celine." "How do I know that?" she asked, with a smile.

"You know already," he said, in a reassuring tone, as he kissed her on the cheek. "Hmm, you cheeky man," she replied, as they both burst into laughter. They hugged each other, and she entered her car then drove off. It's obvious that despite repeated rejection from John, Celine didn't at any time suffer broken heart syndrome, she just continued being her cheerful self despite being turned down after making John her muse.

Celine was quite disappointed that this stunt turned into one of those oops moments, and it was as if John pulled the rug from under her feet. Who forgets the man they had a tremendous rush of blood to their head over, and shamefully it ended merely as a crush. John wished it would be best described as a fling that never happened, with that their friendship can remain pure.

Days and weeks later, John and Celine carried on as if those awkward moments never happened.

It was Saturday afternoon; John took Brenda to the movies. After the movies, they went straight to John's house.

"I'm glad to have you all to myself today," John said in excitement. He has his hand wrapped around Brenda's waist as they walked out of the elevator towards John's apartment. Brenda rolled her eyes at John in a very seductive manner and said.

"You've always had me all to yourself, so don't sound as if all you'd all along was just a fraction of my attention," said Brenda.

"I mean having to see you by my side the whole of today," said John. The moment they entered John's apartment, Brenda pulled John to herself and said. "Come here," baby. She gives him a long kiss and the romance continued for a moment until they paused to take of their jackets.

"There isn't any dull moment with you, and that's why I love you so much and miss you each time you aren't by my side," John said, as he helped Brenda take off her Jacket.

"Why don't you get me a glass of wine to put me in the mood?" she asked, as she makes herself comfortable on the sofa. It's like I need a glass of brandy to equally put me in the mood," John said, as he reached for a bottle of red wine. After they each had a glass of red wine, Brenda and John frolicked around John's apartment and spent all day in each other's arms in love.

While Brenda was in John's apartment, Michael went to Brenda's place to see her. Unfortunately for Michael Brenda wasn't home, but the apartment complex where Brenda lives is fringed by cafes, he immediately hurtled into one of the cafes in his bid to escape the rain shower, and then decided to wait for her in the cafe since she wasn't picking up his phone calls.

John dropped Brenda off at her house at about 6.50pm and went back home almost immediately. Michael, though tired of waiting at the cafe, decided to try Brenda's phone one more time before he left at about 7.25pm.

"Hello Michael, sorry for keeping you waiting," she said as she walks out of the shower.

"Hello, are you home?" Michael asked, feeling a bit frustrated.

"Yeah, yeah, I'm home," she said.

"I'm at the cafe opposite your house, and I'm coming over to your place," said Michael.

"Ok," she said as she tries to make herself decent before Michael steps in. "I'm walking down, please let me into the building," he requested. She lets him into the building, and the moment he walks out of the elevator Brenda lets him into her apartment.

"Hey, you're welcome," she said, as he enters the apartment.

"Yeah, I've been calling your phone, but you weren't answering," he protested.

"Sorry about that, I was with John," she said. She then hands him a glass of red wine. Michael tried shaking off the frustration of spending all day at the cafe waiting for Brenda, and even as he tried making the ambience friendly, he didn't stop short of reminding Brenda that the last time he was at her place she didn't treat him well. Brenda stopped suddenly in reaction to Michael's statement.

"No Michael, I treated you well, just that it was late," Brenda retorted, and smiled as she tries to keep things civil.

"Am I assured of better treatment today?" Michael asked anxiously.

"Yeah, provided you don't ask for the impossible," she said. She turned on the TV to keep him entertained and then sat on the sofa that's just opposite the one on which Michael was seated.

"Is getting back with you impossible?" He asked. Michael smiled and then suddenly gave a stern serious look at Brenda.

"You know that's impossible, Michael," she retorted. Michael stood up, and walked halfway towards Brenda, he stopped suddenly then said her concerns are touching and his excuses aren't good enough, but doesn't mean the situation is beyond repair.

Michael sensed that Brenda won't fall for his flattery, and she seems overly cautious of his visit. Yet he proceeded to inform her that people fall in love, and sometimes they fall out of love. In his case, he fell in love with her eighteen years ago and hasn't been able to fall out of love with her. "Why don't you meet me halfway as I've just done?" asked Michael.

"You suddenly think so?" she asked.

"No, it's because I know so," Michael said.

"No, for sixteen years you never looked for me, you just stumble into me, and then you suddenly know so!" she exclaimed, closing her mouth with both of her hands in an expression of surprise. Someone once called love the old devil, not because he's just being a cynic but simply because love somehow has a way of rocking the boat when we least expect it.

After a momentary silence Brenda continued, and reminded Michael they'd it all going, they'd love and they'd everything worked out, but just in a whim he threw it all away.

"I thought it was love, Michael, but you left without even a goodbye," she said, in a cold and loveless tone.

Surprised at Brenda's reaction, Michael looked at Brenda and said she seem to harbour some grudge against him from the past.

"Of course not, you were the love of my life, I tried reaching you, and I wrote you letters but there wasn't a reply to any of the letters. Though, all that's in the past now," she said, and then became a bit emotional.

"I apologise for the past and I take the blame for my lapse in judgment," he said.

"Apologies accepted, we're still good friends and please, Michael, let's leave it at that," she said. Michael walked back to his seat, still holding his glass of red wine to avoid creating the impression that he's a man with unsavoury appetite. Unfortunately, the mist never comes down, and this time it isn't.

"Tell me about this John. "Is he a nice guy? Do you love him?" He asked. "John is a nice guy, and I'm so very much in love with him," she replied. "Head over heels?" Michael queried further, as he listened keenly to her description of John's personality. "Of course, yes, head over heels, I'm completely immersed in love," she replied. Hmm, what can I say? I just don't want to miss out," said Michael.

Michael didn't press Brenda any further for a love reunion but rather settled for the place of an ex, yet remained on friendly terms. After spending time with Brenda on general conversation, Michael left Brenda's house at about 10.pm after failing to convince her to leave John for him.

CHAPTER
FOUR

The Break-up

Weeks later, John took Brenda out on a Friday night dinner.

John and Brenda stepped out of their car and headed for the entrance door. John opened the door to let Brenda in, and they then walked side by side through the reception, as they proceeded to the restaurant.

"I like this place," John said, as they walk side by side holding each other's hands.

"Yeah, this place is beautiful," she concurred. "Do you know what makes this more beautiful?" he asked. Unsure of John's line of conversation, she asked him what it was.

"Look around," said John. Brenda looked around the restaurant, and was startled because she noticed that eyes were on them. "But, why're they all staring at us?" she asked.

"Your fashion signature is great, and you look like a fashion icon, I suppose that's the reason for the attention," said John. He then wraps his hand around her waist again as they made their way through the restaurant looking for a nice spot to sit.

"You said I look like a fashion icon, ain't I a fashion icon? she asked, and smiled.

"Of course, you are. Please pardon my choice of words," he said.

"Stop it, John. You're making me blush," she said and smiled. John then steered the conversation further as he told her she looks ravishing in this her elegantly beaded gown, and her natural dimples blended well with her outfit to bring out the style in her. He continued whispering into her ears as the waiter ushered them to their seat.

"Are you making me blush to prepare the ground for tonight's romance?" she asked.

"What do you think? The atmosphere is perfect," he said as he held her by the hand and showed her to her seat. Interestingly, Brenda has other things going on in her mind.

"At least you know I'm heads over heels about you. So how much do you love me?" She asked, in a whisper.

"So much," John replied. Brenda then jocularly pushed John a bit further asking him to rate his love for her.

"I'll put it at infinity, I suppose, or plus, plus, plus rather. "Seriously, infinity isn't enough," she protested, and then burst into laughter.

"For how long do you want to be with me?" She asked, as she tickles and teased John. He told her he's in this for the long haul and he wants to spend all the days of his life with her, he then gave her a reassuring kiss.

"Good to hear that," she said, with a smile. John became curious over Brenda's line of questioning, he scooped a spoonful of the content of his plate in his mouth but stopped, then turned to Brenda and asked,

"But why're you asking these questions?" asked John. "I enjoy lavishing those privileges associated with being single," she said. John smartly reminded Brenda that she isn't single anymore, particularly now that he has come to sweep her off her feet.

"Oh, as the Knight in the shining armour I suppose?" asked Brenda.

John and Brenda enjoyed their Friday night out, it was a fun-filled night out. After the Friday night dinner, they spent some time listening to live music for about an hour after which John and Brenda drove straight to John's house. Immediately John and Brenda walked into John's apartment holding hands like infatuated adults.

"Where do we start?" He asked, with his hand around her and kissing her.

"I need to go into the bath, and I'm inviting you to join me in the bath," she said, pulling John by the hand.

"This invitation is timely, and I like it," John said, as he follows her sheepishly. Brenda stopped suddenly, and said.

"Oh, but on one condition."

"What condition? Name your terms," John asked.

"You walk into the bath with your eyes closed," she said.

"Eyes closed? I want this fun to continue all through this week-end," he said, in excitement.

"You already have your wish, because I'm all yours till Sunday evening," she said. John allowed Brenda to go into the bath first, and joined her moments later with his eyes closed as they had fun playing their little game.

John woke up, and began dressing for church in his usual fashion while Brenda remained in bed, though awake.

"Guess what, John?" she asked, as she turned around towards John, with a smile. "You're coming with me to church," he guessed, yet still focused on getting dressed for church.

"No, try again," she insists. "I can't guess, please tell me," he pleaded.

"Ok then, I'm pregnant," she said, in excitement as she got up and sat on the bed. Brenda didn't seem to get her expected reaction from John after broking the exciting news of her pregnancy to him.

"Stop being tricky," John said, without showing any emotion, neither did he pay any particular attention to Brenda who was sitting on the bed.

"Of course not, I've been saving the good news for today," said Brenda. "You've been here since yesterday, and you're telling me this now that I'm almost leaving for church?" He asked, questioning her motive.

"Because I think now is the best time," she said.

"You can't be pregnant, Brenda. That can't be," he muttered.

"Are you being serious? Tell me you're joking," she said. Things quickly became intense as Brenda expressed her frustration and feelings of disappointment in an outburst of anger.

"I'm not ready for a fight this morning, as you can see I'm going to church," John said, trying to keep things calm. Brenda finds John's comment to be hypocritical for saying he's heading off to church when he hasn't addressed the obvious.

"Seriously, what do you take me for?" she asked. She then got up from bed and stood facing John, who's trying to avoid eye contact.

"I never implied anything," he said.

"Are you doubting me?" she asked.

"I mean, what doctor did the test?" He asked, facing Brenda who's already agitated by his disappointing reaction towards her exciting news. "I did the test myself on the morning of Friday," she retorted.

"What if the pregnancy testing kit is faulty?" John asked further.

"You must be joking, and what are you afraid of, John?" she asked, as she rushed towards the wardrobe where her clothes are hanging. John realised Brenda is incensed by his betrayal and insensitivity, and now tries calming her down. John's hesitation isn't because he's unreliable, neither is it because he isn't man enough, but because he panicked over the fact that his parents are conservative Christian and will frown that he's introducing his fiancée to them when she's already pregnant.

"Calm down, Brenda. I don't understand this pregnancy thing, but we'll talk about it when I come back from church," he pleads with her. "How dare you, John? You can't walk out on me," she said. She then picks out her clothes from the wardrobe and began dressing up.

"But I've to go to church, and we'll talk about this when I come back," he said. Brenda confronted John as she told him his Christianity stinks, and that if truly he's a Christian as he claims then he shouldn't have eaten the forbidden apple. She felt betrayed and told John she's leaving, and asked him not to bother checking on her. Even as John tried to press her to stay behind and wait for him to return from church, she hurriedly left his apartment.

"Why're you flouncing off? Come back, please," John said, as he chased after her, to make her come back, but she's having none of it.

After Brenda angrily left John's house, John stayed back and decided not to go church, as he kept trying to get his head around sorting things out with Brenda. Sadly, from the moment Brenda got home she sobbed all through the day. John tried so hard to reach her through the phone so many times, but she wasn't picking up. John then drove to her house, but Brenda didn't let him into the building.

John was quite distraught over his inability to get through to Brenda who finds his attempts to fix his mess to be sort of patronising. He stood in front of the building pressing the bell repeatedly for Brands to let him in, and funny enough, she knew it was John yet turned her back on him. After a while, John gave up and turned around to leave but just as he takes some steps to leave, a resident who had a key to the building and returning from work opened the door to let himself in, and John quickly took advantage of this stranger's magnanimity to let himself into the building. He smiled and said providence is on his side as he quickly used the lift to the 12th floor where Brenda lives and in a jiffy, he's by Brenda's door. He knocked and knocked until his knuckle hurts, Brenda didn't respond either, and to avoid being seen as creepy by unsuspecting neighbours who share the same floor with Brenda, John decided to tuck his tail and leave after his last-ditch attempt to save the day failed.

He returned to his car and drove back home, but while on his way home, the stress precipitated by his kerfuffle with Brenda seem to be intense, and he then slowed his car down as he suddenly felt he needed fresh air. He parked his car in the nearby park, and walked into the park, then sat on one of the wooden benches in the park as he reminiscence about how his day started and how things bizarrely went out of hand and deteriorated so quickly.

He struggled to understand how the woman by his side when he woke up that day is now suddenly estranged and out of his reach. He serendipitously failed to forget that humans are inherently flawed, and that this flawless beauty, that kept him company the previous night could turn her back on him in such a casual but defiant manner.

The weather is sort of windy, with a little gust, this is a bit more than the fresh air he wanted, yet he remained seated until a homeless man sitting on another bench adjacent to where John was seated needed to take cover from the wind, he then stood up to leave but beckoned on John to protect his eyes from the wind that suddenly became boisterous.

John looked around and suddenly realised he's alone in the park after the homeless man sitting adjacent that created a false sense of hope that there are lots of people in the park left. Interestingly, in a twinkle of an eye, after the homeless man left, a pigeon that cared less about the weather flew onto the bench John sat on, it looked at John and began to coo. John suddenly became attached to this lovely uninvited guest that has come to keep him company. He tried reasoning out what this pigeon was going on about and suddenly came to the bizarre conclusion that this pigeon is telling him to go home that everything will be just fine.

Moments later, while the pigeon was still keeping him company, John stood up and walked to his car and returned home.

The next morning, which was Monday, she went straight to her office to submit her resignation letter to her boss, Mr. Whittaker.

Brenda walked into her office wearing a dark pair of glasses to mask the emotional emptiness within as she wasn't looking her usual cheerful self. Moments after she walked in, she opened her bag brought out her resignation letter, and walks straight to Mr. Whittaker.

"There's something about your disposition today, and you aren't looking your usual cheerful self. Is anything the matter?" He asked.

"Nothing really, but I'm resigning my appointment," she said, sounding depressed and cold.

"What's the problem, and why the haste?" He queried further, wanting to know why his usually reasonable and calm employee would resign hastily without the courtesy of a notice of resignation.

"Nothing, I just want to return to the United States, and I need to do this now," she said.

"Is anything the matter? Your look tells me something isn't right," said Mr. Whittaker. He then stood up from his seat, and drew closer to her, trying to understand what the problem was.

She seems not to be having it as she refused being talked out of resigning her job, she told Mr. Whittaker that she wants to go back to the United States, and it must be today, and she then pleaded with him not to try talking her out of this.

"Ok, keep the letter with you, sleep over your decision, and if you want to go through with this resignation, then you should bring the letter to me by noon," he said, trying to give her room in case she change her mind.

"I've thought this through and I've made up my mind. Please take it," she said, as she pressed him, to cut her loose. This isn't a lady tricked into a concocted love-hate relationship presented in some beautifully wrapped package, she's a scorned woman who will not acquiescence anything short of her expectations.

"Brenda, you've been like a daughter to me, if there's a problem we can talk about it," he said, as he tries to assure her he's there for her. She insists it's personal but stopped short of letting out too much about her kerfuffle with John.

"Is it relationship? Or did you lose someone? I've known you to be a fun-loving person," he asked.

"No, I didn't lose someone, but I insist, and please don't be mad at me," she begged him.

"I'm already mad, Brenda, but not at you, at whoever has caused you to be this sad," he said. Interestingly, Brenda is very much a hands-on employee, and Whittaker loved her for that. "I'm booking my flight for today, please just take it," she said. "Ok, if you say so," he said. He took the letter from her, and then continued. "But I'll keep this letter with me, for one month, to help you think things through," he said.

"Ok, thank you," she said. She immediately walked to her desk and partially emptied her drawer, then turned around and waved one big good bye to her colleagues in the open office, she did this with a big smile that masks her mood, and then walks away.

David who originally has a good and cordial working relationship with Brenda got the hint from Whittaker that Brenda is leaving. He felt the need to hear Brenda out, as he opened the door and ran after Brenda.

"Wait a minute, Brenda," David said.

"Yeah David," she said and stopped to attend to him.

"Whittaker just informed me you're leaving us, did you get a better offer in the States?" he asked, curiously.

"Of course not, I just need to deal with some personal stuff, going on," she said. "You can't leave your job over personal stuff, you can take time-off and come back," he said, holding her hand as he tried persuading her to reconsider her decision. David pressed on her and reminded her that the sudden decision to resign her job out of the blue, without even saying a proper goodbye is brash and unnecessary. She stood statue-still for a minute and then withdrew her hand from David.

"Sorry David, but I've to do this," she muttered.

"You know we're a team, and I can't function properly without you, so why don't you take a day or two to give this a thought?" said David. She apologised to David and told him she's sorry if her decision has a knock on effect on him, but she really needs to do this.

"Ok, but just sleep on it," he said, as he presses her further not to leave.

"Thanks, you're a true friend, and I'll give you a call," she said, as she gives him a hug, then turned around and left.

That Monday night, Brenda booked a flight for the Tuesday morning, to Houston in the United States, but by evening of the same day David called Brenda to check on her.

"Oh David, how're you, and what's up?" she asked.

"I'm cool, Brenda, I'm just checking on you," David said, cautiously, as he tries not to engage her on the need to reconsider her decision.

"I'm fine, and that's kind of you, David," she replied.

"Are you sure you're ok and do you want me to come over? he asked, expressing concern for her.

"Don't be silly, David, I'll be just fine and I don't need babysitting," she said, as she burst into laughter.

"Ok then, but are you still travelling tomorrow?" He inquired.

"Yeah, I've booked my flight already and it's the first tomorrow morning," she replied. From her response, David realised her mind was made up, and any conversation persuading Brenda to do otherwise, won't yield any positive result.

"Ok, enjoy your trip, and just give me a call when you reach your destination," he said. She thanked David for checking on her and they said good night to each other and she then dropped the call.

Brenda decided to call her elder sister, Sharon, to inform her she will be coming to the United States, and to possibly share her grief with her.

"How're you doing, Brenda?" Sharon asked her little sister.

"I'm fine, how're you?" she asked, in a low and cold tone.

"You aren't sounding alright to me, err... are you ok, Brenda, and how's John?" asked Sharon. Funnily, Brenda didn't answer the question concerning John. She continued with her dead cat strategy and just went straight on to inform Sharon she's coming over to the States the next day.

"Are you ok?" she asked again with some emphasis because Brenda doesn't seem to be letting out much information about her state of mind. "We'll talk about it when I come over," she said, assuring her sister, she's got everything under control.

"Is it John?" Sharon asked further.

"Yeah Sharon, but we'll talk about it tomorrow," she stressed, still not letting the cat out of the bag.

Sharon's desire to hear about John unwittingly increased as she seeks to know what the problem with her sister was. Brenda on the other hand, didn't tell her much about what the matter was except for the fact that John is the reason behind her sister's stress. Interestingly, this was the only hint she gave out. Sharon decided to give John a ring immediately she ended the phone call with Brenda.

"Hello Sharon, how're you?" he said, in a very mild tone, as he suspect's Sharon's call was more about telling him off as opposed to exchanging pleasantries. "I'm fine, John. Brenda just called me now, and she isn't sounding ok," she said. "She called you?" He asked, curiously trying to salvage the situation. He then continued. "But I've been trying to call her all day and she wasn't picking up," he said. Without giving much time for pleasantries, she immediately went straight to the point and asked him what he did to her sister.

"Nothing, of course! We only had a little argument and that's all," said John.

"You mean nothing? My sister isn't psychotic, John," she queried, sounding unconvinced by John's response.

"Yeah, nothing serious I suppose, I even went to her house, but she refused to allow me into her apartment," he said, as he tried justifying he's a caring person.

"Ok then, I'll get back to you," she retorted. "Ok, thank you," John replied.

John continued to call Brenda's phone but she still wasn't picking up. He then decided to meet her up in her office on Tuesday, but only met her colleague David, and her boss Mr. Whittaker in the office. Sadly, the moment John walked into the office he was met with an empty seat as Brenda no longer works in that office and he was also met with stern looking colleagues of Brenda who suspected he'd a hand in her debacle. Her colleagues took sides with her but remain passive because they obviously have no dog in this fight.

"Good morning," John said, looking startled in front of Mr. Whittaker, whose attention was fixed in the file before him.

"Yeah, morning," David responded from his end of the office. John decided to walk up to David, who's sitting opposite Whittaker.

"John, how're you?" David asked.

"I'm good," said John. "You don't seem good to me, because you're here even when it isn't actually the usual lunch time," David replied.

"Please, where's she? I'll be fine when I see her," said John, as he sat opposite David. Interestingly, David knew who it was John was talking about, yet he unwittingly continued to string him along by giving him the run around in their conversation. John is now looking like the Grinch, and he definitely will need a lot of luck this time.

"Who?" David asked, trying to hear from him, while pretending to know nothing about his issues with Brenda. "Brenda, of course," said John.

"Sorry, John, she resigned yesterday," said David. John was open mouthed as David told him his supposed fiancée has resigned, and sadly, David gave John the news without emotion and didn't share in his despair.

"What? You must be joking," he said. "She should be on her flight to the United States," David said, looking apathetic, as he stood up to attend to a customer who just walked into the office.

"Why would she do this to me? John queried in exasperation. Funnily, John's reaction attracted Mr. Whittaker, who raised his gaze at John and asked.

"What did you do to her that made her look so moody?" he asked. Unsurprisingly, John unwittingly maintained his deniability. "Nothing, it's just a little misunderstanding, but she has taken it too far," John replied.

"Are you sure it's a little misunderstanding?" Mr Whittaker asked, taking off his glasses to get a proper eye to eye contact with John.

"Yeah," said John.

"Her disposition speaks differently, because she doesn't seem to take whatever the problem is lightly," Whittaker explained. David interjected from his end of the office not minding he has a client in front of him, and urged John to keep trying her phone, maybe she'll pick up because he'd hate to see her leave. David's show of support was quite encouraging for John.

"Please, if you can reach her, let her know I've been trying to reach her," John pleaded. John then decided to rush back to his office after a disappointing visit to Brenda's office. Funnily, just as John stepped out of the office, David followed him from behind.

He then called John aside and said he's not used to butting into other people personal affairs but he just had to advise him that he mustn't lose Brenda because he will be the one to lose. John seem not to be overly fond of people who speak in codes, but he'd to avoid fighting on multiple fronts, he allowed David to finish speaking before urging him to give some flesh to his message.

"Why, is there something you want to say to me?" asked John.

He then hinted John that years back when he and Brenda started working together, he realised she is all sweet and easy going and the ambience around this girl is always warm. He then thought to himself that this lady must be masking her dark side with this her smiley, smiley face, and that's when he started waiting for the thing, the moment, and he waited for long.

"What thing, were you waiting for?" asked John, as he tried to convince himself that David isn't sniggering at him.

"Easy, John! I'm not talking about something dirty, except the content of your heart is dirty," David retorted.

"But what's the thing, or the moment you're going on and on about?" asked John.

The thing he was waiting for is actually that moment or time rather, when Brenda will put her sweet and easy-going disposition aside and lash out, get mad at colleagues or even clients, when the real Brenda behind these smiles will come roaring. Funnily, he has waited for that moment until late, and it never came because she maintained her easy going nature and even became sweeter as the days go by.

He proceeded to confess that whatever John must have done to her that got Brenda this upset must have really touched her nerve.

Brenda's characterization as the lady with the sweetest temperament is also now in sharp contrast to what John got from her, and his conversation with David seem to be an eye opener that meant he didn't make mistake going after Brenda.

John became sober as David gave him a brief profile of Brenda, but the sweet story about the woman who is about to become his wife made him more determined than ever to get Brenda back. He then excused himself from David and continued to his office.

CHAPTER
FIVE

Revisiting the Past

Brenda arrived at her late parents' house in Houston to join her sister Sharon. Unfortunately Sharon wasn't able to pick her up from the airport, so she took a cab from the airport to her sister's place.

"Hey, Brenda, good to see you," Sharon said, as they hugged each other the moment she opened the door to let her into the house.

"Good to see you too, oh, I like your hair," Brenda said, as she touches her sister's hair to feel the texture of her hair.

"You've always liked my hair, and I've done nothing new to my hair," she said, as they walked into the living room.

"Where's everyone?" asked Brenda.

"My kids have gone to school and my husband is at work," she replied. While the two sisters were catching up, Sharon quickly turned the kettle on for a cup of coffee for Brenda but Brenda interjected and hinted Sharon she prefers a cup of hot chocolate as opposed to coffee. Sharon knew that coffee is her sister's favourite hot drink but didn't know why she suddenly opted for hot chocolate instead. "Thank you," Brenda said, as she makes herself comfortable with her cup of hot chocolate.

"Tell me all about it, is it John?" Sharon asked as she drew close to her sister and sat by her side to hear more about what the matter is.

"Yeah, I'm pregnant, Sharon," said Brenda.

"Ok, but what's the problem?" Sharon asked curiously as she positioned her ears to listen to what her sister has to say.

"He doesn't seem interested in the baby," Brenda said, and became emotional as her facial expression reveals the despair within her.

"He isn't interested, or he doesn't seem to be interested in the baby, which of them?" Sharon queried further, wanting to know the fact of the matter.

"I can feel it in his tone," she replied as she sobbed uncontrollably. "Don't worry, everything will be fine, John has been trying to reach you," Sharon said, as she consoles her sister with words of hope. Interestingly, Brenda didn't hesitate to reiterate her position in the matter as she made it clear to her sister that John shouldn't be trying to reach her, but rather should be committed to the baby. Sharon on the other hand is a conservative Christian who holds her Christian values dearly. "Mum has always warned us about being pregnant before marriage," Sharon retorted, as she tried to bring perspective into the situation at hand. Interestingly, Sharon's admonition came as a stinker to Brenda who didn't hesitate to remind her big sister she didn't come over to the United States for Sharon to moralise her situation by telling her about her Christianity or any crap. Brenda emphasised to her sister that she needed some respite and needed a break from John, that's why she left. She then turned away from her sister, fixing her gaze on a childhood photo of her and Sharon hanging on the wall. The sisters are now deadlocked, yet Sharon is keen to see a head way.

"I'll take you to Reverend Karl, you need to see him," Sharon said, as she realise their conversation is now deadlocked.

"I don't need Rev. Karl, I need John," Brenda said, as she sobbed the more and her eyes flooded with tears.

"You'll get John back, I promise you. I'll help you get him back," Sharon said, as she wraps her hands around Brenda and comforts her. "I love him, I love him," Brenda said repeatedly, while still sobbing. "It's ok, things may have hit the rock bottom, but we'll steer this ship back to its course once again," Sharon said.

Moments later, Sharon was able to calm her sister with some comforting words. Few days after Brenda's visit, it's now Sunday morning; Brenda visited the Baptist church in their neighbourhood where her parents worshipped when they were alive. She actually grew up in this church, and her parents were committed members, and consequently almost every member of the church knew Brenda and her sister. Immediately after the church service Reverend Karl walked up to Brenda.

"Hello Brenda," he said, with an expression of surprise on his face.

"Reverend Karl!" She exclaimed.

"I recognised you, as you walked into the church. It has been a while," the reverend said. "Yeah, and how're you, Reverend?" asked Brenda.

Interestingly, this beloved reverend that's overly fond of Brenda's parents is now old and grey.

The reverend knew what Brenda used to be like even though it's been long they set eyes on each other, and realised she's far from her usual disposition. He's also aware she left the faith after her parents' demise.

"I'm fine and as you can see, my child, you don't seem happy, but I know God brought you here," he said as he welcomed her and sat by her side for a one to one conversation.

"Reverend, God didn't bring me here; I walked into this church myself with my two legs," she replied, with some emphasis in her tone. He then stopped speaking to allow her vent, and then chatted with her for a while to know more of what it was that troubles her.

The Reverend then steered the conversation into her relationship and asked her about John, and then asked if John is a Christian, Brenda hesitated but then said John is a Christian, and his parents are pure, pure Christians. "I mean traditional Christian," said Brenda. The reverend sensed a thawing in her disposition, and took advantage of it to introduce God to her. He then handed his Bible to Brenda and asked her to open the bible to Jonah 1:4-5, Brenda collected the bible but didn't open it, the reverend however proceeded with what he'd to say.

Just like Jonah who'd wanted to do his own thing by running off to Tarshish, the Reverend reminded her that God used the ship wreck to make Jonah do the right thing, and likewise, God in his wisdom have used this disagreement with John to bring her back to Christ.

The Reverend however made it clear that his questions about John isn't intended to peel her away from John, as he puts on the demeanour of a man who wants to repair as oppose to rebuke. He then reminded Brenda that her parents and John's parents are both conservative Christians but then expressed his disappointment on how John claims to be a Christian yet gets his fiancée pregnant even before marriage. Brenda remained mute and somewhat disinterested as the reverend gave her words of admonition.

"God used your disagreement with John to bring you back to Himself. I'm aware of your parents' prayers concerning you and your sister Sharon. All God just did, is honour His commitment to your parents. He promised to hold you and Sharon close and He just honoured that commitment," said Rev. Karl.

"Like God's commitment to David concerning Solomon or what?" She asked.

"Ooh you still remember your bible," said the Reverend, who then proceeded to say, yes, God promised not to take the throne away from Solomon as a promise to David, and thankfully God just gave her the same opportunity, in His bid to honour his promise to her parents. The reverend did a very good job in his attempt to let Brenda understand what parents' banked prayers can do in sustaining God's promises concerning their children.

Brenda seem to have heard an earful, and asked the Reverend not to lecture her about God's plan because if God does have a plan for her, John and her wouldn't be having this trouble. She did all she could to explain away the words of admonition coming from the reverend.

The Reverend listened but then urged Brenda not to conflate God's plan with God's love because they're different, saying God's love is always available but our obedience is the only thing that will help God's plan to materialise in our life. People walk out on God, do their own thing, and make mistakes just as she has just done, but returning to God to make things right is the right thing to do. "He has brought you here, the rest is up to you, take His hand and He will make you alright again," he said. But made it clear in no uncertain terms that she will have to recommit to God by accepting Christ as her Lord and Saviour, and she will have to do this by her own confession. Again the Revered then asked her to open the bible to the book of Luke 15:11, Brenda didn't, and this time she handed the bible back to the reverend. The reverend smiled and proceeded to suggest to her that just like the prodigal son that left and returned to a father who received him with open arms, God is here to receive her, "He allowed this disagreement between her and John because He knows she will run to her sister and eventually come to the church, and this is God's big plan concerning her life.

Brenda listened but wasn't contributing. "My child, God loves you," he said, as he continued speaking to her. Sadly, his pep talk seem not to be working because she's having none of it and interjected immediately, as she didn't hesitate to ask him if God loves her, why then should He allow her life to be miserable and even allow bad things to happen. She suddenly turned to the reverend and said she doesn't even know what she's doing here. "My child, the truth is, bad things happen to good people but if you lean on God, He'll see you through them all," the reverend said.

"But, why me?" she asked.

"I know, why you, and why shouldn't it be somebody else? Hmm, Brenda, I'll visit you tomorrow at the family house," said Reverend Karl. He then said he suppose that's where she's staying, so she can tell him all about it.

"Ok then, thank you," said Brenda. She put up a brave smile as she stood up from her seat, and then hugged the reverend before leaving to join her sister, Sharon, who was waiting for her.

The next morning, Rev. Karl went to the house to see Brenda. Immediately after the brief exchange of pleasantries, Sharon was quick on her feet to get a cup of tea with some cookies on the side ready for the reverend, and she then stepped aside to allow the reverend some time alone with her sister. She told him about her relationship troubles, and how she left everything behind in London and returned to Houston.

"Reverend, I trusted him, I saw him as different from the others, as nice, compassionate, and as a man with a good heart and actually he is, but I don't know what went wrong," she said, as she pours her heart out to him.

"You see, don't take this the wrong way, but pregnancy before marriage isn't right, it could result in a lot of difficulties and it isn't the Christian thing to do," the reverend said, holding her hand and looking into her eyes as a way of establishing a connection and trust.

"I'm already pregnant, what should I do?" she asked, and she looked straight into the reverend's eyes. The reverend emphatically asked her if she wants John back.

"Yeah, I love him," she confirmed. "Then why did you leave?" he queried further. Brenda replied to the reverend that she expected John to do more, and to show more commitment, and interestingly, her conversation with the reverend is beginning flow better and she's now speaking in a much calmer tone. "My child, sometimes we don't always get what we want," he said, as he tries to confirm the facts of life to her. Sometimes when we do things our way, no matter how good our intentions are, complications do arise, and that's why the Bible emphasised the importance of marriage with the bed undefiled," the reverend emphasised.

"But I'm not asking for too much, am I?" Brenda retorted in a tone that represents her modest nature.

"I'll pray with you, and I want you to trust God with this matter," the reverend said.

The reverend then prayed with Brenda, he prayed to God for his intervention in this matter, and particularly prayed for God to reveal himself to Brenda.

"Thank you, reverend, and sorry about my outburst yesterday," she said, as she tried to relieve herself of the guilt of her hostility from the previous day. The reverend then proceeded to inform her that there's a movie he wants her to watch before their next meeting. He urged her to watch it and let it build her faith in trusting God with her relationship. "I'll send it across to you tomorrow," he said, as he stood up to leave.

"Ok, Reverend, I'll definitely watch the movie, and thank you for your help," Brenda said in appreciation, as she and her sister walked the reverend to his car.

The next morning, Reverend Karl sent the DVD of the movie to Brenda. He also accompanied the disc with a book of the same title, and interestingly, she watched it over and over again, and suddenly began trusting God wholeheartedly to heal her relationship.

Michael had accepted his fate over his interest in winning Brenda back as he decided to keep things civil and preferably remain on friendly terms, but as he usually does, he checked on Brenda in her office but was greeted with an empty seat. Michael then approached David who initially thought Michael came to close a deal on a property he's looking to buy, but he inquired about Brenda and was told that Brenda had quit her job, without any clear explanation.

"I'm here for Brenda, her desk looks dry, and where is she?" asked Michael.

"I thought you've come to close the deal on the property in Chelsea, but if you're here just for Brenda, I can tell you she's fine. Funnily, David didn't hesitate to ask. "Why the sudden craze for Brenda?" Michael was surprised at David's choice of words and wants to know why David will describe his inquiry about Brenda as craze.

"What are you talking about?" asked Michael. David stood up from his seat to explain himself better, but before he did, he first cleared his throat.

"First John, now you, though, never mind," said David. Michael understands that Brenda and John are in a relationship and has no qualms about John inquiring about Brenda, but his concerns lies with her empty desk. "I get you David, but why isn't she in the office?" asked Michael.

"Ok, if you want to know, she quit her job just days back," said David. The news of Brenda's resignation didn't sit well with Michael as he curiously wants to know the reason behind her sudden decision to resign her job.

"Why did she quit her job, and has she gotten something better?" asked Michael.

"I don't know, but she seems to have some issues with her boyfriend and relationship issues, I suppose," replied David.

"How serious is this matter that'll make her quit her job?" asked Michael. "I don't know, because she didn't say," said David. Michael's ear tingled as he hears of the rift between Brenda and

John, and felt the need to check on her to understand the seriousness of the rift.

"Ok, I'll check on her later today," said Michael.

"I don't think so, said" David.

"What do you mean?" Michael inquired further.

"She left for the United States last week Tuesday," said David. Interestingly, Michael and Brenda grew up in the same neighbourhood, he knows Brenda's siblings and knows he could either find her siblings or find her in her family home.

"If she's in the United States, then I know where she will possibly be," said Michael. "Where will that be?" asked David.

"It must be in her parents' house. I suppose, you're aware we grew up together," said Michael."

"Ok, see you next week," said David. Michael is glad in his heart about the rift between John and Brenda because this is an opportunity to get Brenda back. "Ok, see you then," said Michael.

In a matter of two weeks John's social life deteriorated. His colleagues at work noticed a sudden change in John's lifestyle in recent days, making them sense he has broken up with his girlfriend. It was blindingly obvious that he now joins his colleague for lunch and even returned to the old habit of staying late at work. In one of the work days, Philip drew closer to John to inquire what the matter was.

"Are you ok, John?" asked Philip.

"I'm ok" John said and chuckled.

"Are you sure? Because you don't actually look ok to me, said Philip," John tried to dismiss Philip's concerns by trivialising his observations about him, but sadly, John's relapse was quite obvious to all who knew him. Lucky for John, his colleagues aren't the scornful types, and he has no need worrying about them sniggering behind his back.

"Don't worry, I'll be fine," said John. "You stopped staying late in the office about four months ago, but you now join us for lunch at the cafe and stay late in the office," said Philip. John didn't have any further excuse to put forward this time, he unwittingly told Philip he isn't wrong in his observations but he'll be fine. Philip perceives John's response as a partial acceptance that he isn't ok, but didn't stop short of emphasising he will be fine in no distant time. Philip decided to probe further by inquiring about Brenda because the telltale signs that their relationship is strained are there. Philip drew much closer to John to make their conversation more personal.

"How's Brenda? I suppose she's ok," asked Philip.

"She's fine," John assured. Celine overheard Philip's conversation with John even though they were speaking in quite a very low tone, she then stood up from her seat and walked up to John and threw her hand around John's shoulder.

"John, did Brenda leave you, or what?" asked Celine.

"Brenda didn't break up with me, and neither did I break up with her. We'll be fine," John assured. John stood up from his seat as he took Celine's hand off his shoulder.

"Should I come over to your house, to help you through this? I don't mind," asked Celine.

"That isn't what I need right now," said John, with a smile. "Then what do you need, John?" asked Celine.

"It's Ok, Celine. John said he needs some time to straighten things up," said Philip.

In one of the afternoons in the week following, John and Celine are serendipitously alone in the office while other colleagues are out and about dealing with their clients' businesses. There's this air of silence in the office, not because John and Celine aren't on talking terms but because John perhaps was consumed as he leafs through the documents in a file on his desk. He had to attend to this file belonging to a client whom he finds insufferable, and this assignment is already falling behind schedule.

Sadly, Celine has chosen this moment to turn on her charm, and she walked around accentuating her hips as she paraded the office pretending to search for a client's file in the cabinets in the central office. She did that for a while, and sensing that John didn't take notice of her, she then stopped and gazed at John for a while and told him they would've been good together if he'd stopped to see what he'd by his side all along.

John's burst into laughter and his response to Celine's was sort of evasive, and it's obvious that John will never even acquiescence making Celine feel unwanted. As far as John is concerned Celine is an open book, a lovely soul, a work colleague, a dear friend, and a mate, sort of, and letting her down lightly in a manner that won't irk her further is the only option in John's playpen. Realising that John has chosen to be evasive Celine didn't hesitate to join in John's laughter that quickly turned into hysteria. John has always been warm and friendly towards Celine even as he maintained an aromantic ambience around her. Celine on the other hand perceived John as a scared little boy too afraid to take a plunge into the deep.

Yet, she wondered about where John's love for her went, may be through the window, or there wasn't love in the first place.

By the night of the same day, and after work, John lay on the bed as he reminisced about his good moments with Brenda, he then decided to call David to inquire if they've been able to reach Brenda. "Hello David, how're you?" asked John. "I'm good, John. Have you straightened things up with Brenda?" asked David. John responded saying Brenda is still not picking up his phone calls, and asked David if he has been able to reach her. David could feel John's despair even from his cracked voice as he expressed his helplessness with sorting things out with Brenda.

"Yeah, and I told her you were in the office to see her," said David. "The next time you speak to her, tell her I said she should please hear me out," said John.

"Ok, I'll do that," David promised.

"Thank you," said John. David took steps to help John out with a little piece of advice, as he told John that Brenda seems to be with her sister, and suggests he give Sharon a call. "Ok, I'll do that right away," John promised.

John remained in bed for a while analysing the cost and the benefit of calling Sharon first before hearing from Brenda. He was worried that Sharon's response could be incendiary and this could worsen things for him, but if he's able to speak to Brenda's emotional side and establish some connections with her, then things might be better for him. Funnily, after spending some time doing his permutations, he summoned courage to give Sharon a call. Sadly, Sharon dispensed of every pleasantry and didn't hesitate to hit the nail on the head.

"Hi John, why did you put my sister through all this?" asked Sharon. John tried to exonerate himself from any wrongdoing yet tried not to exacerbate the situation.

"I don't understand, and I didn't do anything wrong," said John.

"Do you know she's pregnant?" asked Sharon. "Yeah, I'm aware," John concurred.

"And you know you're the father of the baby she's carrying?" asked Sharon.

"Yes, I think so," said John who seems to be threading with care in his conversation with Sharon, but his responses seem not to be helping either.

"That's cynical, John. You think so, or you know so?" Sharon queried further.

"I know so?" John said, as he tried to correct his earlier comment. "How come she's pregnant and you didn't show concern, but what are you afraid of?" she asked in fiery tone that's emblematic of a lady fighting her sister's corner.

"I wanted to go to church after she gave me the news, and then she got angry," said John.

"How do you mean?" she asked. John tried to explain further, but sadly, the version of the event he's presenting to Sharon wasn't exactly what transpired.

"She wanted me to remain at home and not go to church, the moment she broke the news to me," said John. Though, Sharon's interest wasn't to make matters worse but to restore her sister's relationship, and obviously the need to get the facts out was pertinent to her. "Do you love my sister?" asked Sharon.

"I love her to bits, but I messed up, and that's why I've tried everything I could to let her understand how sorry I am," said John.

"Are you ready to be a father?" she asked again.

"Yeah, I'm ready to be a father, because I'm the father of her baby," John assured Sharon.

After her conversation with John, Sharon sensed that everything is falling back into place but the only aspect of her sister's life that she's still in doubt about, is her job. That also needs fixing if she's to return to London to continue her life. The next day, Sharon called Mr. Whittaker to help secure Brenda's job.

"Hello, good morning," said Sharon.

"What can I do for you today?" asked Whittaker.

"My name is Sharon, Brenda's elder sister," said Sharon, as she introduced herself.

"Oh, how's she?" asked Whittaker. "She's fine. Please, I want to ask you for a favour," said Sharon.

Concerned about what favour Sharon might be asking for, Whittaker paid more attention to Sharon to know what the favour is about.

"Ok, what favour?" He asked.

"Please help me keep Brenda's job" Sharon pleads.

Without any hesitation Mr. Whittaker heaved a sigh of relief and adjusted his tie.

"Is she coming back?" asked Whittaker. "Yes, she'll be back, and she told me a lot of nice things about you," said Sharon.

"She did?" asked Whittaker.

"Of course, she did. She told me you promised to keep her job for a month and that's a kind gesture," said Sharon. Whittaker loved the complements as he smiled at Sharon's appreciation of his kind gesture.

"Yeah, I'll keep her job," said Whittaker.

"She'll return to her job within the one-month grace period," said Sharon. "Good to hear that", said Whittaker. "You're a good man, and thank you very much Mr.....," said Sharon. He quickly interjected, to help Sharon with the pronunciation of his name.

"Whittaker, Ok, thank you," said Whittaker.

By the weekend of that week, Brenda bought some flowers from a florist and visited her mother's grave. She placed some of the flowers on her mother's grave and began to sob by her graveside, talking to her dead mum.

"Mum, I know you can hear me. I know you and Dad are Christians and I kind of did things my own way, but now I'm back to say I'm sorry. Over the years I saw this Christianity thing as crap, but now I get it. I'll equally apologise to Dad," said Brenda.

Brenda then turned to her dad's grave and placed the rest of the flowers on his grave, and began to sob, saying the same words she said by her mother's graveside.

The day after her visit to her parent's graveside, Brenda visited the church to see Rev. Karl. She waited behind after church to see the reverend.

"Hello Rev.," said Brenda.

"Hello, my child, you look brighter. How're you doing?" asked Rev. Karl.

"Yeah, I just want to thank you for everything, you've been quite helpful," said Brenda.

"I've been praying for you, and I've asked God to encounter you," said Reverend Karl.

This time Brenda's disposition was affectionate and her cheerful nature was in full glare as her infectious smile precedes her conversation with the reverend. "I visited my parents' graves, to apologise to them for doing things my own way and I've felt so good since then," said Brenda. Although, Rev. Karl didn't think visiting the grave to speak to the dead is a Christian thing to do, he though, appreciated her willingness to set things back on track.

"I thank God for you, my child. Has John called you?" asked Rev. Karl. Brenda smiled at the reverend's questions as her facial expression explains her emotional attachment to John.

"Actually, he has been trying to reach me, but I'm just taking my time," said Brenda. Reverend Karl smiled and encouraged her further. "Just continue trusting in the Lord, everything will fall into place, piece by piece," said the reverend.

"Hello Rev," said Sharon, as she walks into the conversation, the reverend then turned to Sharon.

"Your sister is looking brighter than ever," said Rev. Karl. "She's fine now, and everything will be alright soon" said Sharon.

Days later, Sharon felt the need to cement things up between John and Brenda but felt it's time to for Brenda to open up to John and talk things over with him. Sharon went to the garden where Brenda was seated enjoying the scenery of the green vegetation on the other side of the pond behind her parent's house.

"Have you heard from John," asked Sharon. "Yeah, he has been calling, but I've not been picking up" said Brenda. Sharon wasn't happy with the way Brenda was stretching this, and believes her prolonged silence could exacerbate the strain in their relationship. "Why?" asked Sharon. "You know why," replied Brenda. "He has been trying to reach you, and he has even been to your office a number of times, what else do you want?" asked Sharon. "He should try harder" said Brenda.

Interestingly, Michael decided to return to the foray as a wild card, and this time decided to travel to the United States to see Brenda. He went to her father's house to check on her, but finds her in the company of her sister, Sharon, as they return home from the church. When Sharon saw Michael walking towards them, she gazed at him for a moment trying to recollect his face because there was a flicker of recognition.

"Isn't that Michael?" exclaimed Sharon.

"Yes, I am, and it has been quite a long time," said Michael. Interestingly, Brenda wasn't expecting company.

"Hey Michael, you're meant to be in London, I suppose?" asked Brenda.

"Yeah, but I happen to be here, and decided to check on you," said Michael. The sight of Michael brought Brenda some emotional relief as she couldn't stop laughing from the moment she set her eyes on Michael.

"Oh my God, Michael, it's been sixteen years, I suppose. How're you, and how's your mum?" asked Sharon.

"My mum, she's fine," said Michael.

"Sorry about your dad. Brenda told me he passed on," said Sharon. After few minutes of catching up, Sharon excused herself to allow Brenda and Michael to do some catching up of their own, knowing that Michael was Brenda's teenage flame, she left them behind to join her kids in the house. Even as Brenda laughed with Michael, she was rattled and pondered how Michael knew she was in the States.

"Michael, how exactly did you know I'm here?" asked Brenda.

"I checked on you in your office, and was told about you and John," said Michael. She tried divorcing her emotions from the situation to help her avoid making a poor judgement.

Michael is quite an assuming personality, and pandering to Brenda in moments when her relationship was heading for the rocks is his best big move ever.

"And you decided to travel all the way to the United States to see me?" asked Brenda. Michael stood statue-still for few seconds trying to get the best response to Brenda's question, "a man is as good as his word" Michael replied. He then proceeded to say that, "love looks not with the eyes but with the mind, and therefore is winged cupid painted blind."

"Oh, William Shakespeare!" exclaimed Brenda as she burst into laughter.

"Is it bad to show concern for my first love?" asked Michael. "What do you want, Michael?" asked Brenda. Michael felt the need to hit the nail on the head, as opposed to beating about the bush, since Brenda wasn't wavering in her questions. "Since you and John have broken up, can we come back together?" asked Michael.

"That isn't happening, Michael. For your information, I'm pregnant for John," said Brenda. Thinking that the mention of her pregnancy will make Michael back off, Brenda realised that the news of her pregnancy came as a surprise to Michael but his determination didn't shrink.

"Oh, really? But I don't mind, I'll take care of you and the baby," said Michael.

"Oh, Michael, what do you take me for?" Brenda protested.

"I don't mean any harm, Brenda. I'm only expressing my love for you," said Michael.

"Seriously, are you for real?" asked Brenda.

Brenda's stance seemed to be too poignant for Michael, who isn't overly fond of being let down, particularly for a man with a big personality as himself. His ego has just been bruised and as a way of managing his emotion, he had to clasp his suit with his hand. Funnily, Michael's wandering eye speaks volumes, and his relentless disposition tells it all, but this time he might have to back off for good, and forever.

Realising his trip to the United States is like riding a horse that isn't willing to drink from the river and effort to convince Brenda is like flogging a dead horse. He'd to find a way of not making himself look like a creep, and just that life has a way of slapping us in the face sometimes.

"Look, Brenda, I'll benefit nothing, squabbling with the woman I hope to make me happy," said Michael.

"John and I have settled our differences, and we're back together," assured Brenda.

"You mean there isn't a slight chance for us?" asked Michael. At this point of the conversation, the rejection was beginning to get to Michael, as his broken voice reflects his frustrations.

"I don't hate you, Michael. Just that I'm already with somebody else before you showed up" said Brenda.

"Ok, but don't tell me to give up trying, because I won't," said Michael.

Moments after his failed effort to win Brenda back to himself, Michael walked into the house to see Sharon and her kids before saying good bye. Brenda then walked Michael to his rental car, holding hands with him as a way of keeping things amicable. They then stopped by the car and chatted for a while, before she gave Michael a hug and they wished each other good bye.

In one of the evenings, John returned from work and was lost in thought all alone, as he lay on the bed thinking about what precipitated this cocktail of chaos and about his failed attempts to reach Brenda. He decided that the only way to get himself out of this pickle is to reach Brenda through her sister Sharon. John jumped out of bed and decided to put a call across to Sharon.

"How're you, John?" asked Sharon.

"I'm fine, and how's she?" asked John.

"She's fine," said Sharon. "Please, can I speak to her?" asked John.

"Yeah, there's nothing stopping you," said Sharon.

John was elated by Sharon's response, as his hunch tells him today is the day he has been waiting for.

"She isn't picking up my calls, and can I please speak to her through your phone?" asked John.

"Ok, let me hand the phone over to Brenda" said Sharon. She then walks to Brenda and hands her the phone.

Brenda took the phone and was silent on her end of the phone even after John said hello repeatedly to her from his end of the phone. This time is different because before now, each time John called in his bid to straighten things up, Brenda will pick up but won't even think it wise to fob him off, she just allowed John to tire himself out by allowing the phone to ring forever. The fact that he wasn't fobbed off by her seems to suggest she likes the little game she's playing with him.

Convinced that the person on the other side of the phone is Brenda, John began speaking.

"Brenda, you know very well that I love you. Please talk to me," said John". Brenda still remained silent on the phone as John tries to pacify her. Yet, John continued, "you know, you're the light that gave my life a direction. I still want to attend the walk on the runway with you; you showed me the life out there. I'm about to go to bed and all I need to sleep well is your laughter. Just laugh and make me happy," said John.

Brenda burst into laughter, and John joins her in the laughter and they were both caught up in the hysteria.

"Thank you for your laughter, Brenda. I'll call you tomorrow to apologise unreservedly for whatever wrong I've done," said John.

The next day, convinced that Brenda has stopped giving him the run around, John decided and called Brenda's phone directly, and they made up over the phone after John tendered his unreserved apology to Brenda and promised to visit her in the States to bring her back to London where she belongs.

CHAPTER
SIX

The Reunion

That same day John requested a few days off work, and booked a flight for Houston the next weekend. He landed at the George Bush Intercontinental Airport as early as 6.50pm where Brenda was already waiting in the arrival lounge at the airport, with Sharon and her kids waiting at the airport car park. Brenda was quite eager to see John and she was already seated in the lounge waiting despite an estimated arrival time of 7.35pm. On sighting John, Brenda rushed to welcome him; she gave him a hug, kissed him, and sobbed.

"Oh babe, it's good to see you," said John.

"Hey, it's good to see you too, I missed you, and I love you so much," replied Brenda. She began to sob ecstatically the moment she drew closer to John and gave him a hug.

"It's ok, you know I love you, and you're my breath of fresh air," said John.

"You're making me blush. Let's go, Sharon is waiting," said Brenda.

"You mean Sharon is here?" asked John.

"Yeah, she's waiting in the car," replied Brenda.

"Ok, let's go," said John. They held each other by the hand as they walked to the car park to meet up with Sharon who was waiting.

"Oh John, is that you? Welcome," said Sharon.

"Yeah, thanks a lot for helping out, and how're you?" asked John.

"Of course, we're fine and it's good to finally meet you," said Sharon. John and Brenda sat at the back seat of the car making jokes, tickling and giggling themselves as they drove straight to Sharon's house.

As they entered Sharon's house, Sharon's husband walked to the balcony to welcome John.

"John, meet my husband, Kane," said Sharon.

"Hello Kane," said John.

"Good to see you, John," replied Kane.

"Thank you for having me," said John. Kane followed them from behind as they walked into the house, while still holding a conversation with John.

"How's London?" asked Kane. Sharon and Brenda left John with Kane to continue their conversation while they set the table for dinner.

"London is busy as usual," said John. Interestingly, while they were both alone, Kane steered the conversation into personal stuff, as he turned to John and said.

"We don't know each other much, John, but I think I'm in a better place to advice you," said Kane.

"I know I've created a bad impression of myself, even before you met me," said John.

"I know, but Brenda is a good girl who never allowed her beauty to overshadow her choices," said Kane.

As the conversation continued, Kane became more personal with John, because he felt no love would be lost between them if he tells him the truth.

"I actually love her, but I've been a fool," said John. "A fool about what? She took her time to pick you out of crowd," said Kane.

"About how I handled the news of the pregnancy," said John.

"A real man is known for his show of commitment and his ability to take responsibility," said Kane.

"I know, I cowered away, but I promise to live up to the expectation of everyone," promised John, but in his heart, he knew that this rollercoaster of events was precipitated by his fear of how his parent will perceive him.

"I know you're a Christian, but how good a Christian are you?" asked Kane.

"It's hard qualifying one's faith, but I consider myself a good Christian," said John.

"If you are, you shouldn't be having sex before marriage," retorted Kane.

"Yeah, I get it," said John.

"What's done is done, though, you're welcome again. The table is set, let's go and have dinner," said Kane. They both stood up from the sofa where they were seated and moved to the dining room and chatted as they ate their meal. After dinner, John retired to Brenda's room.

"I'm sorry for whatever I may've done to you, or in whatever way I may have treated you poorly," said John. He proceeded to confess to her that he unwittingly panicked at the news, but that does not in any way mean he isn't ready to be a father, and at least he'd loved the idea of being called dad by a toddler.

"That's in the past now, let's focus on the future," said Brenda."

"The future? Then you're going back with me, the day after tomorrow," said John.

John and Brenda spent most of the night catching up, as they lay in bed with their arms wrapped around each other enjoying the comfort of each other's warmth.

"Why are you in a hurry?" asked Brenda. "I've come to take back what belongs to me," said John.

"What's it that belongs to you and aren't you objectifying me?" asked Brenda.

"Sometimes a little objectification can be a good thing, some say. You, and my baby mean the world to me," said John.

"Ok, you're beginning to sound convincing," said Brenda. John felt at home as things fell back into place between him and Brenda. The emotional void he felt since Brenda's departure suddenly disappeared, and he's now beginning to feel like the man of the hour. Interestingly, John was also quite elated with the ecstatic reception he received from Brenda's relatives, after all there wasn't anyone kicking off over his poor treatment of Brenda.

"You know I've to go back to work," said John.

"The day after tomorrow will not be possible, what about my travel ticket?" asked Brenda.

"I'll book your flight, right away." said John.

"Let's pray," said Brenda. John was surprised to hear Brenda suggest prayer, because his previous conversation with her suggests she didn't fancy religion.

"Pray? I don't understand. How come you suddenly became interested in prayers?" asked John,

"I rediscovered myself, on my return to the United States," said Brenda.

"Which means, we're now on the same page, but your fire seems to be much more than mine," said John. They both laughed.

"Ok, let's pray." said Brenda. They prayed and continued chatting all night until they eventually fell asleep.

The next morning was a Sunday morning. Sharon walked in on Brenda and John as they had their breakfast at the dining table.

"John, is that what you're having for breakfast? asked Sharon. "Yeah," said John. She immediately turned to her sister and asked why John is having cereal for breakfast and not a proper breakfast.

"That's what his appetite craves, ask him," said Brenda.

Sharon's felt it'll be better for John to meet with Rev. Karl to discuss how Brenda and John could solidify their relationship for the best, particularly now that pregnancy is involved.

"John, Brenda will take you to see Rev. Karl," said Sharon.

"Who's Revered Karl? I mean, who is he to you?" asked John.

"The man behind the new Brenda you see," said Sharon.

"Really! I would love to meet him," said John.

"Yeah, he helped me come to terms," said Brenda.

"Come to terms with what?" asked John.

"God's love for me, I suppose," said Brenda.

"When do we meet him? You know our flight to London is tomorrow," asked John.

"You can see him today", assured Sharon.

"When today?" asked John. "Today's Sunday, you guys should go to church," said Sharon.

"Ok, we'll see him later today," promised John. "No, it's best to see the reverend immediately after church," said Sharon.

"Ok, immediately after church is the best option then," said John.

John and Brenda attended church service and waited behind to see Reverend Karl immediately after the church service.

"Hello Reverend," said Brenda. John and Brenda drew closer to the reverend, the moment he finished speaking to an elderly couple immediately after service.

"Hello my child, how're you doing?" asked Rev. Karl.

"Reverend, meet John," said Brenda.

"Oh John, good to see you," the reverend said, in quite an ecstatic tone.

"Good to see you, Reverend," John replied.

"How's London and how was your trip? Come with me" said Rev. Karl. The reverend took John and Brenda to his office for a private chat, and when they got to his office, the reverend asked them to make themselves comfortable and took a moment to make them coffee, but Brenda declined taking coffee or tea.

"Brenda told me about you, and about everything," said Rev. Karl. "Oh, Ok! John exclaimed" "Are you a Christian, John? I mean, have you surrendered your life to Christ? asked Rev. Karl. John hesitated because he knew what the reverend meant by being a fully surrendered Christian, and his present antecedent is a far cry from what that meant.

"Hmm, yes I have," said John.

"Do you love Brenda?" the reverend asked further.

"Of course, I do!" John exclaimed.

"Do you want to spend the rest of your life with her?" the Rev. asked.

"Yes Reverend," said John. John's initial expectation was that his meeting with reverend Karl was about a casual exchange of pleasantries and wasn't expecting his meeting with reverend Karl to involve discussing his intimacy with Brenda. John eventually loved the direction flow of the conversation, as it means Brenda is now his to have and to love. The reverend then turned to Brenda to get her position on this matter.

"Brenda, what about you, do you want to spend the rest of your life with him?" asked Rev. Karl.

"Yes, Reverend," said Brenda. "Then I'll not take much of your time, you both know sex before marriage is wrong, and when it results in pregnancy, a lot of problems come with it," said Rev. Karl. John interjected.

"I'm sorry about that, Reverend. The pregnancy wasn't planned," said John.

"Apologise to God, not me. Now that this has happened, you need to get married and live officially as husband and wife. That'll be a more honourable approach before God and man," said Rev. Karl.

"Yes Reverend, we'll get married, and we'll do that soon," said John. The reverend insists on John and Brenda genuinely giving their lives to Christ, and take their Christian faith seriously, which they eventually committed to.

"Ok, good to hear that," said Rev. Karl.

"Reverend, we'll call you and inform you of the day and time," said Brenda.

"I want to thank both of you for choosing to do the right thing," said Rev. Karl.

The next day, Sharon and her husband Kane dropped John and Brenda off at the airport as they depart to the United Kingdom.

"Let's walk them to the departure lounge, and wait for them to board," Kane proposed.

"I don't think they need our company," said Sharon.

"How do you mean?" asked Kane.

Sharon laughed and jocularly said John and Brenda have each other and three could be considered a crowd in this case.

"Which means we're on our own," said Kane.

"John should keep Brenda company, and Brenda should do likewise and keep John company," said Sharon. They all burst into laughter over Sharon's suggestion as they unload their luggage from the car.

"Ok, I wish you a safe trip," said Sharon.

They walked a few steps forward and stopped, Sharon hugged Brenda then moved over to John and gave him a hug as well.

"Thank you. You've been wonderful to me," said John.

Kane also gave Brenda a hug then moved over to John and gave him a handshake.

"I wish you all the best," said Kane.

"Thank you, Kane. Your family has been wonderful," said John. Then they walked in and boarded their flight and departed for London.

Brenda and John returned to London from the United States on Monday, and by Tuesday Brenda was in her place of work.

"Hello, you're back, and good to see you," said Mr. Whittaker from his desk. David interjected as he stood up and gave her a hug.

"Oh Brenda, you're back, good to see you," said David. Brenda walked to Mr. Whittaker's desk and stood in front of him.

"Err.., I want to thank you, for everything," said Brenda.

"You're thanking me for what?" asked Whittaker.

"For keeping my job, and I truly appreciate your kind gesture," said Brenda. Mr. Whittaker tried playing down his kindness towards Brenda, by not assuming the role of a hero in all this.

He responded by saying this is nothing, and it's what a friend or a father can do for a loved one.

"You guys are like my family now," said Mr. Whittaker.

"I know my relationship issues are personal, and I'm sorry for rubbing it off on all of you," said Brenda.

"Ok, glad you're back, and that's what matters. How is your sister, Sharon?" asked Mr. Whittaker.

"She's fine, and she extends her greetings," Brenda replied.

"You're a lucky girl, having her as a sister," said Mr. Whittaker.

"Yeah, I'm truly blessed," Brenda replied.

Brenda turned to David after she finished speaking with her boss. David smiled and said his heart is just healing from the shock of her supposed sudden resignation. She immediately tapped David on the shoulder and said she's back now. David continued his line of conversation, saying they're a team and are like two peas in a pod, when you've two peas in a pod, and one suddenly disappears, it leaves the remaining one in limbo. "I know you're back, that's why I'm talking about healing, and that's because the shock stage is over," said David. Brenda laughed, and then thanked David for checking on her, and for being not just a colleague, but a friend.

John returned to the lifestyle he was leading before the break-up three weeks earlier. Though, his colleagues at work had no idea he has sorted things out with Brenda. "John, wait for me, so we can go for lunch together," said Philip. "I don't think so, because I'm going somewhere else for lunch," John replied.

"Are you sure you're ok? Or is Brenda back?" asked Philip. "Mate, I'm cool," said John. "What's happening, and does this have anything to do with your taking a day off work?" asked Philip.

"I took a day off for personal reasons, but you might be right about Brenda and me," said John. While the conversation with Philip continued, Celine interjected.

"John, is she back?" asked Celine. John opened the top drawer of his desk and placed some files inside as he tidied his desk then stood up from his seat. "I'll respond to your question when I come back from having my lunch," said John.

After lunch John brought Brenda to his office to let his colleagues know they are back together for good and also, to formally introduce her to Tom Bradley.

"Hello," Brenda said as she walked into John's office holding his hand. "Oh, I sensed it, and I said it, Brenda is back," said Philip. John stood in the middle of the office still holding hands with Brenda, and he then turned to Celine who's sitting at her desk.

"How come you guys read my every move so easily? Celine, I promised you when I return from my lunch break, you would get your answer," said John.

"You've just answered my questions with actions as opposed to mere words, I suppose," said Celine.

"Yeah, and I'm sorry for the secrecy, but I feel it's time we make things more official," said John. Philip stood up from his seat, walked up to John and Brenda where they stood in the middle of the office and gave Brenda a hug. "Welcome back," said Philip. Celine fixed her gaze on Brenda and said.

"How're you? We've been worried," said Celine. "About what?" asked Brenda.

"We thought you guys had gone your separate ways forever," said Celine. Sadly, Celine's comment precipitated a change in Brenda's disposition because she finds it troubling. Arguably, Brenda finds Celine's comments to be anything but a sort of relentless sarcasm but this isn't enough to bring about paranoia that wouldn't look good on both ladies either.

"Isn't that a bit harsh?" Brenda retorted.

"Of course not, we were truly worried for the both of you, but he hasn't given us any explanation," Celine explained. Philip noticed the conversation has gone sour following Brenda's reaction to Celine's comments and tried to tone the conversation down a bit. "I don't want to know what happened, but thank you for coming back to John," said Philip. Celine added her voice and said John has been moody for some time now, and seeing Brenda again, will bring back some brightness into John's life.

"Guys, for your information, we're getting married," said John.

"Oh, when?" asked Celine.

"We don't know yet," said John.

"Good to hear you're taking things to the next level, and I'm happy for you, mate," said Philip.

"I'll inform you guys of our plans," John assured them. "Thanks for your concerns for John, I mean for us," said Brenda.

"Please let me introduce her to Tom," said John. Sure, go ahead," said Philip. Interestingly, now that all the topsy turvy is over and everything seem to be falling right back into place, John is now confident to inform Tom about his plans. Moments later, they entered Tom Bradley's office, and funnily, Tom initially thought Brenda was a client but became confused when he noticed they were holding hands.

""Yeah, John, what's up?" asked Tom. "Tom, this is Brenda, my fiancée," replied John, as he held hands with Brenda. "Hello Tom, nice to meet you," said Brenda.

"Hello Tom, nice to meet you, said Brenda.

"Hello, you're welcome, and good to meet you too," said Tom. Unsurprisingly, Tom Bradley stood up from his seat and gave Brenda a handshake, then turned to John.

"You've chosen correctly, John. Is your office around here?" Tom asked Brenda.

"No, my office is near London Bridge," said Brenda.

What are they into? asked Tom.

"We're estate agents," said Brenda.

"Thank you for bringing your fiancée to see me, John, you did well," said Tom.

Brenda thanked Tom for the warm reception and said John has said a lot of nice things about him, and funnily, Tom is business minded but this time he gave in to some sweet talking as he turned to John with a smile.

"Is that true? Some months back, I noticed a change in John's lifestyle, then I realised he hasn't just found a woman, but he has found a good one," said Tom.

"Tom, I'll inform you of our plans soon, because we'll be getting married." said John.

"Oh, you guys are getting married? That's good news!" Tom exclaimed.

"Thank you, Tom," said Brenda. "She has to go back to her office," said John. Tom thanked Brenda for the courtesy of coming to see him, then said he hopes to hear of their plans soon.

John and Brenda left Tom's office then said goodbye to his colleagues before dropping Brenda off at her office.

That evening John felt the need to inform his parents of the new development with Brenda, while still eating his dinner. He picked up his phone to give his mum a ring but decided it's best to put the call across the moment he finished eating his dinner to inform his mum that he and Brenda are coming over to see her in Yorkshire.

"My son, how're you?" asked Maggie. I'm fine, Mum. What about dad, and how's he doing?" asked John.

"Your dad is fine, and it's 7.30pm, John. Are you still in the office?" asked Maggie. John burst into laughter to make light of Maggie's concern the moment his mum steered the conversation away from pleasantries to her usual line of questioning of where he's at.

"Why're you always asking if I'm in the office?" asked John. "Because I needed to be sure you haven't gone back to your old ways, and remember, you were still in the office when I called last week," said Maggie.

"Why're you so keen on knowing my location each time we talk on the phone?" asked John. "You aren't under surveillance, and I'm only asking because I care about my son," said Maggie.

"Ok, I'm home and just felt I should give you call," said John.

"Thank you for the phone call but what about Brenda? I told you I would want to speak with her," Maggie retorted.

"She's not with me here, but I'm bringing her to Yorkshire to meet you and Dad," said John. Maggie smiled the moment John talked about their planned visit to Yorkshire, meaning her much anticipated meeting with Brenda is being fulfilled.

"When are you doing that? I can't wait to meet her, but have you seen her parents?" asked Maggie.

"Her parents are dead," said John.

"Oh, sorry about that," Maggie apologised.

"But I've seen her big sister, her name is Sharon." said John.

"When did you do that and is her sister with you in London?" asked Maggie. "No Mum, she's in the United States.

"Did you travel over to the United States to see her sister?" asked Maggie.

"Yes Mum," said John. Maggie muttered saying his son has been busy all these while.

"Then you must be very serious about settling down, and I'm happy for you, my son," Maggie said ecstatically.

"Thank you, Mum," said John.

"Then when are you bringing Brenda to see us?" asked Maggie.

"We'll be coming over at the weekend, possibly on Saturday," said John.

"Ok, we'll be expecting you," said Maggie as they said good night to each other.

At the weekend, John took Brenda to see his parents in Yorkshire to introduce her officially and also inform them of their marriage plans. Unsurprisingly, Maggie was already at the door to open for them the moment they knocked.

"Hello Mum," said John as Maggie opened the door.

"Good to see you, my son, and you must be Brenda," Maggie said, as she turned to Brenda.

"Of course, I'm Brenda, and how're you doing, Mother-in-law?" asked Brenda. The mention of mother in-law by Brenda was quite soothing for Maggie, she liked it.

"I'm fine, and you can call me Maggie, but you look so pretty," said Maggie. John's dad, Jim, walked into the living room the moment John and Brenda stepped into the house.

"You're welcome, Brenda. It's good to finally meet you," said Jim. "Thank you, and good to finally meet you too" said Brenda.

Brenda's pregnancy is less than two months old, and there's obviously no baby bump to show she's a couple of months gone. John understands his parents are conservative Christians, and would prefer to keep the news of Brenda's pregnancy under wraps, lucky enough she doesn't look it. Keeping secret of this nature is like setting oneself up for failure, particularly when dealing with an experience hand like Maggie.

An hour after their exchange of pleasantries, John and Brenda settled in as they made themselves comfortable. They spent some time catching up, but it didn't take long after their arrival that Jim asked John to come with him on a fishing leisure trip.

Jim was all dressed up in his fishing gear and looking ready to go, "John, I'm going fishing, and I want you to come with me," said Jim. John seems to think that this call was a social call.

"Yes Dad, but, what about Brenda?" asked John.

"Leave Brenda with your mum," said Jim. Unsurprisingly, Maggie knew there's more to this surprise leisure fishing trip than a mere catching up, and so, she quickly went along with Jim's plan.

"You have to go fishing with your dad, and allow the women to do their thing," said Maggie.

"Let's go, John," Jim said. "What do we go with, the car or the bicycle?" asked John. "We're going in the car," said Jim.

Moments later, after Jim and John left for fishing, Maggie stood up from her seat, and walked towards the kitchen and then stopped.

"Brenda, I want you to give me a hand in the kitchen," said Maggie.

"That'll be nice," said Brenda as she stood up and followed Maggie from behind to the kitchen.

"Can you help me make these spring rolls?" asked Maggie.

"Ok, I like this town, it's quiet and serene" said Brenda.

"How often do you go to church?" asked Maggie.

"Actually my parents are Christians," said Brenda.

"What about you?" asked Maggie. Brenda had to confess that before now she didn't go to church, but she recently had an encounter, and presently, she can boldly say she's a Christian. This visit opened her eyes to the realisation that John' parents are conservative Christians. Maggie and Brenda connected with each other quickly, as they chatted about life and everything. Maggie stopped speaking, and subtly, asked Brenda how many months gone she is. Maggie wasn't being suggestive, she was direct and somehow this question did more than take the wind out of Brenda's sail, as she struggled to give a fitting response to Maggie. She'd to come clean, and Maggie jocularly told Brenda John should know better.

"I want to tell you a story," said Maggie.

"A story? Ooh, I'd love to hear it," said Brenda. Maggie stopped what she's doing and began telling her story.

"I was 17 when I joined my parents for a cruise ship holiday to Italy; the ship docked at the coast of Sicily. I was standing on the dock and was looking at the sea, when a handsome man, a 22-year-old trainee engineer on board the cruise ship, walked up to me. "My lily, can I show you around?" he said. He took me by the hand and showed me around the ship, and then we ate Ice cream together. When we returned to England after the holiday, he took my address and promised to write me a letter. We continued writing to each other, and I treasured his letters so much, that I usually kept them under my pillow, so I could dream of him in my sleep. One day I was working in the garden, when someone said "My lily." I turned around and it was him. When spring came, we got married. Forty years on, I'm still in love with Jim. This is my story, if you tell yours forty years from now, I hope you'll tell it laughing," said Maggie and continued with what she was doing.

"I pray for a happy ending, and I look forward to it," said Brenda.

"My son is a good man, and with a good heart," said Maggie.

"John also told me a lot of good things about you; he took his good nature from you, I suppose," said Brenda.

"I know little about you, but something tells me you're a good girl," said Maggie.

"Thank you, it feels good to hear that," said Brenda. Maggie stopped what she was doing again and turned to Brenda, looking right into her eyes.

"What're your plans for the wedding?" asked Maggie.

"It's going to be a small church wedding, or do you want us to hold the wedding here in your church in Yorkshire?" asked Brenda.

"It depends on you, my dear, if that's what you want," said Maggie. Brenda remained silent for a moment.

"In your story, you said you and Jim got married in spring. Why do people love getting married during spring?" asked Brenda. "Spring represents a new beginning, it represents regeneration, it represents fruitfulness and for some, it represents second chance.

"Oh, I love spring," Maggie said with a smile.

Meanwhile Jim and John were at the riverside, fishing, they spent most of the time catching up, particularly about John's child hood memories, and after a while Jim steered the conversation into a new area of philosophy.

"Do you know the qualities that make a fisherman unique?" asked Jim.

"I know fishermen are good at catching fish," said John.

"No, they're patient, they're attentive, and they've respect for the fish," said Jim.

"Learning about the qualities of fishermen is good, but their patience is what usually stands out," said John.

"This isn't just about the fisherman its how it relates to you," said Jim.

"Is there any relationship between me and a fisherman? Or there's something you want to say to me," asked John.

"Now you're about to become a husband, and then a father," said Jim as he dropped the line in the river and then focused on John.

"Yeah," said John.

"Then you must be patient, attentive to your wife's feelings, and you must have respect for your wife," said Jim.

"Oh, now I get the relationship with the fisherman!" John exclaimed. "Forget the relationship, but focus on the qualities," said Jim.

John's dad continued to lecture him on the qualities expected of him as a husband, a father and most importantly a Christian throughout their recreational fishing expedition. John is now made to understand that marriage is an assignment and a place of perpetual indulgence. It was quite a Father-Son time out and John actually enjoyed every bit of because it made him reminisce his childhood years when he often spend time with his dad by the river, fishing.

John and his dad, Jim, returned home after three hours of fishing. Aside the marriage counselling session, the father-son fishing experience is something they enjoyed quite well because they both missed the experience.

"Hello Mum," said John. He then walked into the kitchen.

"My son, you're back?" asked Maggie.

"Yes Mum, time with dad was quite an exhilarating experience and it reminded me of those childhood moments," said John.

"Your dad has missed those father and son moments with you, I suppose. He saw an opportunity and he took it," Maggie said.

"No, mum, this was actually a lecture class," said John. Maggie gave Jim a kind of look with her side-long glance that speaks volumes following John's comment and they all burst into laughter as John dipped his hand into his bag to bring out their catch.

"Oh, you caught some fish," said Brenda.

"Yeah, and how're you? You're having a catch up with my mum, I suppose," said John, as he drew close to Brenda in the kitchen. Interestingly, Brenda has been doing some thinking because she has something else in her mind. She nibbled into John's ear and said his mum knew about the pregnancy, and John suddenly opened his mouth and asked to know how it come about that his mum knew. She hinted him that his dad is equally aware, and somehow they just know about it, but went on to ask "what if we have our wedding in a church, here in Yorkshire?" asked Brenda.

"Is it you suggesting this, or my mum?" John queried.

"This is me suggesting, and this isn't your mum," said Brenda. John seems not to give thought to Brenda's proposal.

"Fantastic, you're making spring rolls, I like them," said John as he dipped his hand in the bowl and took one and began snacking on it.

"What do you think?" asked Brenda.

"About what?" asked John.

"I think I like this place, this town is quiet and serene," said Brenda.

"Ok, I'll discuss this with my dad, so we can see the priest before we leave tomorrow," said John.

After putting their heads together John and Brenda agreed to give the idea of holding their wedding in Yorkshire some thought. John loved the idea of a marriage ceremony in Yorkshire because of the support he'll get from his parents to make the entire process seamless, but most importantly because it was all Brenda's idea.

By evening of the same day, John got a phone call from Philip.

"Mate, how're you doing?" asked John.

"I'm fine but I want you to bring Brenda along for drinks so we can get to know her better," said Philip.

"When?" asked John.

"This evening, I suppose," said Philip.

"No, that won't be possible, maybe next time," said John.

"Why?" Philip queried.

"We're presently with my parents in Yorkshire to further discuss about Brenda and I," said John.

"Oh, that's a good move, maybe next weekend," said Philip.

"Ok mate, thanks," said John.

By the evening of the same day, Jim, Maggie, John, and Brenda were all seated in the back garden of their house, when John's dad brought up Brenda's suggestion of holding the marriage ceremony in Yorkshire.

"John, your mum told me about your plans," said Jim.

"What plans are you talking about, dad?" asked John.

"Your marriage plans, of course" said Jim.

"Ok, we're thinking about having the wedding here in Yorkshire instead of London," said John.

"Will your guests be able to make it to Yorkshire?" asked Jim.

"We don't want the wedding to be large, we just want something small with a few guests," said Brenda. Jim adjusted his seat, in a bid to hear what John and Brenda had to say, yet he has to make sure that whatever plan John and Brenda has in place is tight and rock solid. Jim then told the love birds that they know quite well that Brenda is pregnant, even though the love birds decided to keep mum about it. He then expressed his disappointment in John, and said he needed to ask them one or two questions before they go further into wedding their plans.

"What questions are you asking, Dad?" asked John."

"John, Brenda, are both of you serious enough to want to get married?" asked Jim.

"Yes, we're not kids anymore, to be unsure of what we mean or what we wanted," said John.

"We've already given that a thought, and we're actually in love," said Brenda.

"Lastly, Brenda, I'm sorry about your parents, but have your close relations accepted John?" Jim probed further.

"Oh, I like this line of questions, my big sister has actually met John and she likes him," said Brenda.

After telling John off, for taking the ungodly root to the alter by getting his wife pregnant, Jim called his son a Christian hypocrite for paying lip service to his Christian faith. He then turned to them and said everything is fine and he's with them all the way, particularly now that they desired to fix their error. Maggie interjected as she told Brenda that Jim didn't even know John was in the United States to see her sister, Sharon.

"How would I know, when John only talks to his mum about himself?" Jim protested.

"We're having our wedding anniversary on the 25th of October and that's about three weeks from now," said Jim. While the conversation was ongoing, Maggie stood up from her seat, then went inside the house and moments later returned with some grilled fish on a plate for Jim.

"Oh you grilled some of the fish, that's why I can't stay too far away from home," said Jim with a smile.

Maggie attended to Jim's choice drink, then turned to Brenda.

"Brenda, why don't you go to the grill and get some for you and John?" asked Maggie.

"I'll do that later, we're taking our time," said Brenda.

CHAPTER

SEVEN

The Wedding Bells

Maggie had planned to meet with Father Bill, the parish priest of the church where she and her husband worship in Yorkshire. Immediately after Sunday service, Maggie approached Father Bill to discuss Brenda and John's proposed marriage plans.

"Hello Maggie, how're you today?" asked Father Bill.

"Oh Father, I'm fine," said Maggie as she drew closer to the priest.

"I hope you enjoyed the service,"

"Of course Father, I enjoyed the message, and the service was great. Please, my son will want to see you," said Maggie. "Which of your sons, Maggie?" asked Father Bill.

"I'm talking about John, you remember I told you he now has a fiancée," said Maggie. The priest affirmed with a nod that Maggie did tell him about John, he then proceeded to ask what the matter is about John.

"He's here with his fiancée, they were in church and they're planning to get married," said Maggie.

"I saw someone looking like John sitting side by side a blonde lady, but he looked a bit different," said Father Bill.

"Of course, that's John, they're planning on getting married, and they wish to speak with you, I suppose," said Maggie.

"Ok, I'll see them immediately since they're already in the church," said Father Bill. "But I must inform you that she's two months gone, I mean pregnant. And I've expressed my disappointment," said Maggie. Maggie looked away after breaking the news of Brenda's pregnancy to Father Bill because she knows too well of his conservative views on marriage.

"You know the church doesn't encourage a thing like that," said Father Bill.

"They're in the church waiting to see you, and it'll be a good thing for you to express your disappointment directly to them," said Maggie.

"Where are they seated?" asked Father Bill.

"Over there, the second seat in the second isle by the entrance," Maggie said, as she points to John and Brenda.

"Ok, thank you," said Father Bill.

While John and Brenda were seated, and waiting to meet with the priest after church. Cathy, the younger sister of Tonia, John's former crush whom he pursued years back but failed, saw John and Brenda in the church while waiting to meet with Father Bill. Cathy walked up to John and they exchanged pleasantries.

"Hello John, it's been a while and how're you?" asked Cathy.

"I'm good, Cathy. What's up?" asked John.

"I'm fine, good to see you, and how come you're worshipping with us today?" Cathy probed further.

"I suppose you like the fact that I'm worshipping with you today, and it's an opportunity to see you again," said John.

"Oh, I love it, and who's she?" Cathy asked pointing to Brenda.

"Ooh, meet my fiancée, Brenda," said John. In truth Brenda didn't really like Cathy's probing questions, because her inquiry about her came across as too direct but she'd to keep up appearances for John's sake. "Err..., Brenda, you're welcome and how're you?" asked Cathy. "I'm fine, Cathy, nice to meet you too," said Brenda.

"How's Tonia, your sister? It's been a long time since I saw her," asked John.

"Tonia is in London, and she's fine," said Cathy. "Really? I haven't even bumped into her," said John. Father Bill drew closer while John and Cathy were still holding a conversation.

"I need to meet with Father Bill, he's waiting for us," said John.

"Ok John, I hope to see you around," said Cathy.

Cathy stepped aside to make way for John and Brenda as they made their way to Father Bill who's already waiting for them.

"Hello Father, it's good to see you," said John. "Thank you, John. It's been quite a while, your mum told me you're here," said Father Bill.

"Meet my fiancée, Brenda," said John. Father Bill gestured to show them to his office as they talked and walked into his office, they then made themselves comfortable.

"Hello Father," said Brenda.

"Good to finally meet you," said Father Bill.

"Finally meet me, and is there anything I don't know?" Brenda asked in surprise and smiled.

"I've been aware of you and John for some time now, and I have looked forward to meeting you," said the priest.

"Father, we've come to let you know, we're getting married." said John.

"When do you have in mind?" asked Father Bill.

"Possibly three weeks from now," said John. Brenda interjected quickly before the reverend's comment on John's proposed three weeks.

"We don't want to wait too long because I'm two months gone," said Brenda. Father Bill turned to John, not looking so impressed.

"John, I suppose you know, you missed it," said Father Bill.

"I missed what, Father? I don't understand," asked John.

"Your parents are examples of good Christians in this community, pregnancy before marriage shouldn't come from you," said Father Bill.

"I get it, Father I'm sorry about that, but let's see how I can put things straight back on track," said John.

"Is she a devoted Christian?" asked Father Bill.

"She wasn't before, but she recently had an encounter with Christ," said John.

"Three Saturdays from now is free based on the church calendar," said Father Bill.

"Which means we're free to wed in three weeks' time," John said with an ecstatic smile. The Father interjected and said John and Brenda would need to go through marriage counselling, but unfortunately he isn't sure if the proper counselling can be achieved within the time available them.

"How do we do that? We live in London," asked John.

"Yes, I know," said Father Bill. The priest rummaged through his drawers and brought out two books, and handed them to Brenda and John, then drew closer to them.

"Oh, thanks," said John.

The priest then told the pair that the books he just gave them are on the importance of a lasting marriage and how to achieve it. He then asked them to take one each and study.

"Father," thank you," said Brenda. "I'll call to ask you questions from the book, this book isn't meant for your shelves but to help your marriage blossom, and wax strong," said Father Bill. John unblinkingly promised the priest they wouldn't disappoint him, and after much of the talking, the priest promised to work with Maggie to set things in place.

Father Bill concluded by asking John and Brenda to complete the marriage form to enable the preparation for the wedding ceremony. After about an hour and half meeting with the father, John and Brenda are now on their way out, but as they were leaving the church they bumped into Cathy who seems to be waiting for someone.

"Cathy, you're still here?" asked John.

"Yes John, I'm waiting for my friend, she wants to see the father. Are you done with him?" asked Cathy.

"Yeah, we've to get going because we're returning to London today," said John.

"Good to see you, Brenda," said Cathy.

"Thank you, and nice to meet you too," Brenda said, holding hands with John.

"John, can I've your number?" asked Cathy. "Of course, you can have it," said John. John began reading out his phone number to Cathy, who typed it into her phone contact lists immediately. "Ok thank you, and goodbye, John," said Cathy. John and Brenda walked out of the church premises and continued home. Funnily, Brenda's feminine instinct kicked in, and smelt a rat in Cathy's move as she felt Cathy was deceitfully waiting for John and wasn't actually waiting for a friend, but even at that she remained civil.

"Did you've to give her your number?" asked Brenda. "Is that a problem? We're all from this village," said John.

"Ok, I'm not saying there is," Brenda retorted.

By the night of the same day, Cathy called her sister Tonia, to talk about John. Tonia was John's former crush who never gave John any audience, and neither did she show any interest in John because of his odd lifestyle. John tried very hard for a green light from Tonia but all he got was a no light at all because she never even looked John's way.

"Hey Cathy, how're you and Mum?" asked Tonia.

"I'm fine and Mum is fine as well, but guess what?" asked Cathy.

"Cathy, I don't think I can do this guessing game for now, I have to rush somewhere, to see a friend," said Tonia.

"I saw John! Cathy exclaimed.

"Which John? I know a lot of people by that name," said Tonia.

"Tonia, I'm talking about John Watson," said Cathy.

"Oh my God, you mean John Watson? The boring guy that was falling for me years back?" asked Tonia. Cathy laughed saying of course they're talking about the same John, but the John she just saw is a man with bundle of energy and laughter, and he's quite different from the John they used to know.

During Cathy's brief meeting with John, she noticed a change in John's personality, her hunch tells her that the John she just met is different from the boring man who stays all day at work and eats pizza for dinner after work.

"What do you mean?" asked Tonia. "He came to see Father Bill with his fiancée," said Cathy.

"Why're you trying to mess up my day with this story of a boring guy who obviously is about to marry an ugly or perhaps another boring lady?" asked Tonia.

"Sorry to disappoint you, John Watson is now a very polished man not only in looks but in style, and his fiancée doesn't just look like a model, she looks more like a supermodel, Cathy said, and burst into laughter.

"She can't be as classy as me; at least you know I'm very pretty," Tonia said as she tried to assure Cathy.

"Big sister, from what I just saw, she's classier than you may think," said Cathy.

"How's he able to transform from his usual self to the person you've just described, and to be able to get such a beautiful lady?" Tonia asked in surprise.

"I just told you what I saw. Though, it doesn't matter, because you were never interested in him," said Cathy.

"Don't worry, I'll give John a call later today and see if he's different from what he used to be, and possibly win him back," said Tonia.

"He seemed to be planning for his wedding, and I don't think it'll be proper getting between them," Cathy warned.

In her usual sense of humour, Tonia didn't hesitate to remind Cathy that John used to fall head over heels for her, and if John sees her he will fall and she will get him back.

Sadly, Tonia unwittingly reminded her sister that she will only win John back if he now has style as she just hinted her. Yet, she didn't stop short of a subtle caution that if John is still the same boring John, she will leave him and go her way. Her belittling remark about John's description as some odd guy in the shadows hiding in alleys was quite a characterization that won't help her planned reunion.

Later that day, John and Brenda returned from Yorkshire, and considering the fact that their wedding date is just around the corner, Brenda felt it's time to inform their friends and relatives of their plans.

Before shouting her wedding date to the world, Brenda's first phone call was to her sister, Sharon, as she couldn't wait to inform her sister of her Yorkshire experience, having just returned from her visit to John's parents.

"How welcoming are John's parents and are they nice people?" asked Sharon.

"Yeah, they're very nice people and I see Maggie as someone I can work with," said Brenda.

"Maggie, who's Maggie?" asked Sharon.

"John's mum, of course. With Maggie, there are no dull moments," said Brenda.

"You must be lucky to have Maggie then, and I can't wait to meet her," said Sharon.

"We met the priest and fixed 25th October for the wedding," Brenda said with a smile.

"You mean you met the priest in Yorkshire, but why Yorkshire and why not London?" asked Sharon.

"It'll make the process easier, and his parents have a good relationship with the priest and that's a plus for us," said Brenda. "Ok then, but 25th October will be three weeks away from now," Sharon emphasised. "Yes, please, but I'll have to inform Reverend Karl," said Brenda.

Sharon wasn't quite impressed with the idea that the wedding date is just three weeks away, considering the travel involved. She suddenly became momentarily silent after Brenda urged her to please inform Reverend Karl of her wedding plans. She then asked Brenda if she wants the reverend to attend her wedding in Yorkshire.

"Yeah, I'll send you his flight ticket so you can hand it to him, John and I want him to be a part of the wedding," said Brenda.

"Ok then, I'll have a word with Reverend Karl, and I'll talk to you later." said Sharon.

The next day, Brenda was at John's place after the close of work. She spent some time dotting the i's and crossing the t's, as they worked as hard as they could to put their wedding plans together. She then made dinner, and after having dinner they decided to give Reverend Karl a phone call.

"Hello reverend, it's me, John," said John.

"How're you, what about Brenda, and is she ok?" asked Rev. Karl. Brenda who sat next to John while he had the conversation, interjected the moment the reverend inquired about her.

"Yeah Reverend, I'm fine, and how're you doing?" asked Brenda.

"Reverend, we've fixed 25th of October for our wedding and we want to inform you about it" said John.

"That should be in three weeks' time!" Rev. Karl exclaimed.

"Yes reverend, and we want you to be there," said Brenda.

"Is that really necessary?" asked Rev. Karl. John interjected, in an expression of gratitude to reverend Karl.

"Yes Reverend, we owe this union to you."

Brenda then interjected again saying they'll send the reverend's flight ticket through Sharon. Reverend Karl on the other hand seemed interested in other granular details as it relates to this wedding, as he asked the couple-to-be if they've spoken with a priest about their plans. "Yes, we've spoken with the priest in the church in Yorkshire where John's parents' worship," said Brenda.

"Ok thank you, I'll see Sharon," said Rev. Karl.

After the phone calls, Brenda freshened up and was preparing to return to her apartment, but Interestingly, John seem to have a lot in his mind.

"We're done with the phone calls, it's now time I go home," said Brenda.

"You don't have to, you can stay till tomorrow," said John.

"I need to go home, to be able to get ready work tomorrow," said Brenda.

John stood up and drew closer to Brenda and wrapped his hands around her waist, as he tried convincing her to spend the night in his place.

"You should be thinking of moving in with me," John proposed.

"Why are you in a hurry about that?" asked Brenda.

"We're about to become husband and wife, and moving in should be a part of the package," said John.

"Yeah, but there's still time for that, and no more love making before marriage," Brenda said, as she tried to keep some safe distance from John to avoid the temptations of the flesh.

"Moving in doesn't imply love making," John said, as he tried to assure Brenda they both want the same thing.

"There are temptations associated with living together," said Brenda.

Brenda continued getting ready to leave even as their conversation about the practicalities of moving in with John was on going, she puts on her shoe and grabbed her hand bag and then turned to John.

"Let's assume what happened in the past was a mistake, but it now behoves on us to do the right thing," said Brenda.

"Doing things right, what are you talking about?" asked John.

"No more intimacy for the next three weeks, until after marriage," said Brenda.

"Ok, you're right, it's time to do the right thing," John concurred.

"I'm ready to leave, give me a ride home," said Brenda.

Moments after John returned from dropping Brenda off, he rushed to the bathroom to take his shower before going to bed, but just as he stepped out of the bathroom, his phone rang, and when he picked up the phone it was Tonia on the other end saying hello.

Unsurprisingly, John's courtesy didn't really make provision for pleasantries with Tonia.

"Is it really you, Tonia?" asked John.

"It's me Tonia, and why're you surprised?" Tonia asked in quite a friendly and whispering tone.

"Of course, and to be precise, Tonia, I'm actually surprised to discover it's you on the other side of the phone," said John.

"There isn't anything to be surprised about, because it's been long since I heard from you, and I felt I should call to know how you are doing," Tonia said, as she fiddles with her hair.

John wasn't keen to engage and as such wasn't quite forthcoming, but pressed on Tonia as he asked to know if Cathy gave his number to her because he knows for sure that she deleted his number from her contact list. Tonia isn't new with kissing frogs because she has kissed a few frogs in her short life time but this frog which she seemed to have ignored in the past has suddenly become one that interests her.

Tonia realised that John is sounding cold, she then interjected without any hesitation.

"Why are you sounding like this? I'm just a friend calling another friend to see how he's doing," said Tonia.

Tonia continued in her impressionistic tone as she tried to steer the conversation away from her past treatment of John, but sadly, John wants the past visited and addressed before discussing the present.

"Tonia, I'm sorry and I don't intend to be rude. Did Cathy give you my number? Let's settle that before we move on," asked John.

Yes, I got your number from Cathy, but do you have to crucify me for calling you almost immediately?" asked Tonia. Funnily, Tonia is now struggling to have a proper conversation with John, as things suddenly became tense, and John then decided to tone things down and make the ambience friendlier. Getting over Tonia's betrayal seems a bit difficult for John. The straw that broke the Camel's back for John was the Saturday he saw Tonia in his neighbourhood, and immediately offered to treat her to a surprise brunch in his home. Unfortunately, John's refrigerator was close to empty but he'd to go out of his way to put up a show. An hour later, he had a bottle of Prosecco in his hand waiting for her to walk through the door after quickly cobbling up a strange brunch at the speed of light, yet she seemed unsatisfied to get the afternoon up to speed. She didn't turn up, and that for John was the point he had to draw the line on Tonia.

"Cathy said you've been in London all this while, and funny enough we never bumped into each other," John chuckles. "Actually, yes, just that you never cared to ask after me and that's why you don't know, but how has life been treating you?" asked Tonia.

"I'm fine and life has been good, Tonia. Unfortunately, my fiancée just left and she would have said hi," said John.

Tonia pretended not to hear John's mention of his fiancée, yet continued her line of conversation in her usual whispering tone as if John was still single. He knew for sure he wasn't excitingly loved by Tonia, and crossing path with Brenda was a sign of good things to come, and the best thing to ever happen to him.

"Are you still staying on the 15th floor of that sky-rise building?" asked Tonia. "Yes, I am, but how come you know where I live even though you never visited me before?" asked John.

Unsurprisingly, Tonia steered the conversation into areas John considered grey, and said Cathy gave her a lovely report about him, but asked John if it's true that he's now looking different from the John she used to know.

"I can't remain the boring-looking John that stays late at work and eats pizza for dinner, as you once described me," John retorted in a candid tone. In a very dramatic move, Tonia began to sob uncontrollably over the phone but John became momentarily silent and speechless because he was taken aback by Tonia's shocking emotional display.

"How can you say you love me? And Before I make up my mind to say yes, you've already started another relationship," asked Tonia, as she assumed the place of a victim. John tried wriggling himself out of this sudden drama precipitated by Tonia as he quickly told Tonia there isn't any need shedding crocodile tears or crying over spilt milk. He quickly, reminded Tonia of how she once warned him never to call her," said John. Of a truth, Tonia was blessed by nature with beauty.

"A pretty lady like me should have the pleasure of taking her time before responding to potential suitor," Tonia replied.

"I never held you responsible for taking your time, but I just noticed you didn't have a place for me in your heart," said John.

"We need to get things back on track, John," she said, suggesting she will come over to John's house so they can talk things over. "Please don't. Let's not belabour this matter and I don't think there'll be any need coming over to my place," John protested.

She then insisted, urging John to let her worry about the trouble of coming over and said she'll come over anyway. At least it has been long since they saw each other, before wishing him a good night.

By the evening of Tuesday which is the next day after Tonia's phone conversations with John, Tonia was at the entrance of John's apartment complex waiting for John to allow her into the his apartment.

"Hello, John. It's me, Tonia," she said.

"Tonia? At the entrance of my apartment," John asked, in surprise.

"Yes, it's me, John. Let me in," said Tonia.

"Ok, the door is open, use the elevator and make your way upstairs," said John. It didn't take long before Tonia walked into John's apartment with a smile, but instead of making herself comfortable on the sofa, she gave herself a tour of John's living room.

"Surprise, surprise," said Tonia.

"How are you, Tonia? But you never told me you were coming," said John.

"That's why it's a surprise, and at least you're aware that not everyone enjoys the privilege of having a pretty lady paying them a surprise visit," said Tonia.

Interestingly, John's facial expression wasn't welcoming but Tonia continued her posturing as she ignored John's stern look. After all her mission is more about making an impression.

"As you can see, I'm just coming back from work and will soon be on my way out," said John.

"Ask me to sit down, John. You don't stand a pretty lady up, but I must confess, you look quite different," said Tonia.

"You mean, the boring-looking John?" John asked with sarcasm.

"Of course not, but I'm truly impressed you're looking fine-tuned and smart," said Tonia.

"Oh, thanks to my fiancée, Brenda," said John.

"Between Brenda and me, what's your pleasure? And don't tell me you're choosing this Brenda over me," said Tonia.

"I've chosen her already, didn't Cathy tell you?" John retorted.

Moments later John offers Tonia a glass of red wine only after she made herself comfortable on the sofa and he also gave her some nuts in a saucer to nibble on.

"I like your apartment, and maybe if I consider you for my husband, we'll definitely move because this apartment isn't classy enough," said Tonia.

"Why are you living in denial?" asked John.

While John was still busy trying to wriggle himself out of Tonia's clutches, his phone rang and he excused himself to answer the phone. Interestingly, it was Brenda on the other end of the phone asking if John is already on his way to hers, and her patient is running thin.

"Where're you, John?" asked Brenda. "I'm still at home," said John.

"I've been waiting for you," Brenda retorted. "I'll be about an hour late, please bear with me," John pleads.

Brenda's knowledge of John was that he's never late on a date.

"What came up?" asked Brenda.

"It doesn't really matter, I'll join you soon," said John. "Ok, I'll be waiting but don't be late, and I love you," said Brenda.

"I love you too," John replied. John completely kept Tonia's visit out of his conversation with Brenda, to avoid any possible spasm that might follow in the wake of such conversation.

Tonia frowned the moment she realised it was Brenda on the phone, and sadly, the fight in her came to the fore as she got barefaced and roared at John.

"You mean you chose her over me?" asked Tonia. Sadly, the conversation became a frank one the moment Tonia opened this can of worms, and funnily, John took the bait and didn't hesitate to let the worms sprawling all over the place as he took her down memory lane. "Have you forgotten how I tried so hard to gain your attention just for a minute?" asked John.

"You wanted a minute in the past, you didn't get it. Interestingly, and I'm here now giving you my entire evening. You have my attention, John, what else do you want?" asked Tonia.

"Do you remember the insults you hurled at me, and the names you called me? To add insult to injury, you deleted my number from your contact list," said John.

"I'm a classy lady, and I suppose you weren't expecting me to give in so easily to your proposal?" Tonia asked, as she drew closer to John. John muttered aloud as he reminded Tonia that being classy isn't all about a person's looks but a function of character and style.

"Beauty brings class," said Tonia. John moved away from Tonia to keep a safe distance even as she keeps inching closer to him. John ceased the opportunity to lecture Tonia as he reminded her that there are lots of people out there with pretty faces, yet lack class. He then focused on Tonia and passively told her she's pretty but the character is missing. Tonia felt infuriated over John's comment yet remain calm as she tried to win back the man she never had in the first place.

"Are you returning the insults?" asked Tonia.

"We're only telling each other the truth, you never gave me access to your heart when I was in desperate need of your affection," said John. John finished dressing up and was about to leave the house but conversation with Tonia seems forever, and without an end in sight.

"We can give it a try, and John, I'm here for you" Tonia said, in a seductive tone. John is now feeling like a captive in his own home, and it didn't take long before he began manifesting some emotional irritation towards Tonia.

"That won't be possible, Brenda is already pregnant, and we've just concluded wedding plans." said John.

"The wedding can be cancelled, John, and you don't need to rush into the arms of a woman you aren't in love with," said Tonia.

"I need to go, Tonia. My fiancée is already waiting," John retorted.

"Are you asking me to leave your house?" Tonia protested.

"No, we're still friends just that I've got an appointment," John assured her.

"Ok, but we have to continue this conversation," Tonia said. She stood up from her seat, took her bag and quickly put on her stiletto heels, and then left as John followed her from behind as they both leave the apartment.

Two weeks to the wedding date, John returned from one of his lunch breaks with Brenda, and immediately they stepped into the office, he brought out a card from his folder and invited his colleagues officially to his wedding. "Hello guys, I'm officially inviting you to my wedding," said John. "Wow, wow, finally, my John is taken," Celine said, as she walked towards John and collects the invitation from John, then gave Brenda a hug before returning to his seat.

"You nailed it at last, John, and I'm happy for you guys," said Philip.

John's colleagues passed the wedding invite among themselves, Celine passed it to Lesley immediately she finished looking at the card.

"Congratulations, John, and to you Brenda," Lesley said. After handing the invite to Lesley, Celine looked at John for a while as she fixed her gaze on him. John noticed Celine was lost in thought as she fiddles with her hair, fiddling with her hair is usually what she does unconsciously whenever she's troubled, yet accepted her fate that effort to win John's heart was a lost battle.

Feeling frustrated that John is slipping away from her grip, Celine seem to become more delusional as the day goes bye, yet retained her usual polite and courteous nature in her conversations and dealings with John.

John on the other hand, had to adopt a cafeteria-style approach in his relationship with Celine, at least to avoid his working relationship becoming adversarial.

For all it's worth, Celine isn't some kind of sterile and passionless witch forcing John into her ambit. She's a love sick lady seeking a man of her own but going about it the wrong way. She's quite a lady, overly fond of John, strangely though, she sure leaves a lasting impression.

"Lesley, please pass me the invitation, and let me have a look at it," said Philip.

"John, we'll talk about your plans later, so we know where to come in," said Celine.

"Thank you. What can I do without you guys? Please permit me to inform Tom about it," John said as he walked towards Tom Bradley's office.

The moment John takes Brenda into Tom's office to inform him of their wedding. Tom pointed to Brenda and trying to recollect her name.

"You are..." Tom asked. She cuts in.

"Brenda," said Brenda.

"Sorry, I'm not good at memorising names at first meeting, my bad," said Tom.

"That's not a problem," Brenda said with a smile.

"How're you doing?" asked Tom. "I'm fine, thank you," said Brenda.

"Tom, we've come to inform you of our wedding," said John.

"Wedding? When is it coming up," asked Tom.

"It'll be on the 25th of October," said John. The moment John mentioned the date of their wedding, Tom Bradley quickly grab his diary to check out the suitability of that date, the man is business minded and his business mustn't suffer. Meanwhile, John gave Brenda's hand a soft squeeze as he watched Tom flip through the pages of his diary. This is because he knows that kerfuffle from his chosen wedding date could mean his flawless reputation and his wedding plans could go up in flames if Tom decides to throw a spanner in his way.

"25th of October, you said? That'll be about two weeks from now," Tom asked, after consulting his diary.

"Yes, about two weeks from now," John concurred.

"Where's the venue?" asked Tom.

"The venue will be in Yorkshire," said John. Tom stood up and adjusted his glasses in surprise at John's choice of wedding location.

"Yorkshire, and not London, will that be convenient for you?" asked Tom.

"Yeah, my parents are there, and we want it to be something small," replied John.

"Ok, no problem, we'll be there because you're a committed employee," said Tom.

"Thank you, Tom. You've been wonderful," John said with a smile. Tom's understanding of his staff having a wedding isn't just about the wedding itself but the honeymoon period, and the troubles of getting someone to cover for the newlywed.

"Do you intend to go for a honeymoon after the wedding?" asked Tom. "Of course!" John exclaimed. "Then you'll have to prepare a handover note and handover every case file with you to Philip two days before your wedding date," said Tom.

"Thank you, Tom," said Brenda.

"Tom, she'll be leaving for her office," said John.

"Ok, thank you, and I wish you the best," said Tom. John and Brenda then turned around and left Tom's office.

It's two weeks to the wedding and Brenda perceived that leaving Michael in the dark about their wedding date will spell doom for their fragile friendship. She then decided it's right to inform Michael right away.

"Hello. What a surprise and I hope I'm not dreaming!" exclaimed Michael.

"Of course not, but John and I are getting married," said Brenda.

"What, you mean this your John beat me to it?" Michael asked jocularly.

"I understand your waggishness, but I'm inviting you to my wedding, and it'll be 25th October," said Brenda. Michael continued in his full high-spirited jokes for a while.

"Despite how I feel about losing you, I want to say, this is still good news," said Michael.

"Good to hear that," said Brenda. Michael then steered the conversation away, as he hinted Brenda of his desire to meet John before the wedding, saying he would like to acquaint himself with the man taking his woman from him.

Brenda went silent for a while as she thinks through managing the possibility of a showy display of subtle rivalry between Michael with his big personality and her modest John.

"Why would you want to see him?" Brenda asked, with some scepticism in her tone.

"To let him know you deserve to be treated well," said Michael.

"That won't be necessary, Michael, John knows," said Brenda.

"I don't mean any harm, but I'll need a handshake with him before the wedding," Michael insists.

"Ok then, I'll make sure you get the handshake as requested but I've to go now," said Brenda.

John had always kept Brenda to himself and away from the prying eyes of his colleagues, but now that the wedding bells are about to ring, John decided that it's time to bring Brenda into his circle of friends. Their usual Saturday happy hour is the best atmosphere where she will get to familiarise herself with John's colleagues. John and Brenda then joined his colleagues for weekend happy hour drinks.

"Thank you for bringing Brenda to us, at least we'll get to know each other better, said Philip. "You're right, and she's now part of the one big family," said John. Celine gave Brenda a hug and continued jocularly which is emblematic of her frolicsomeness around her colleagues, as she said this one big family is coordinated and managed by her. After a moment of exchange of pleasantries, they ordered their first drink and they were all drowned in conversation, and interestingly, Celine suddenly steered the conversation away from general stuff into something more personal.

"Brenda, how're you planning for your wedding?" asked Celine.

"We just wanted it small, not loud, and with few guests," Brenda said.

"What church are you using in Yorkshire?" Celine asked further.

Interestingly, Celine has been to Yorkshire a number of times and knows the terrain.

Brenda hinted Celine that the venue is clearly stated in the invitation and it's the church close to the park, and asked Celine if she has been to Yorkshire. "I know that church, I was there about a year ago for my aunt's wedding," said Celine.

Moments later, while John and his colleagues are busy enjoying their happy moment, Celine held up her glass of wine.

In quite a free-spirited tone, Celine enthusiastically raised her glass and said she wants to propose a toast.

They all lifted their glasses of drink.

"To John and Brenda," they chorused, as they merry and laughed all through the evening. This evening time was quite helpful in toning down the subtle rivalry between Brenda and Celine. This is because it was an opportunity for Brenda to find a friend in Celine, as they chatted all evening as if they've been friends forever.

CHAPTER

EIGHT

The Double Wedding

Brenda takes Michael to John's office to see him, and funnily, all Michael wanted is a handshake with the man taking Brenda away from him. Brenda didn't really like the idea of a handshake but she decided to go along with it. As far as Brenda is concerned, this handshake unwittingly represents a truce, but there wasn't a war in the first place, so why the truce. The moment they stepped into John's office, Celine was the first person to welcome them.

"Hello Celine, how're you doing?" asked Brenda. "Hey Brenda, you're welcome." Celine said, as she leaves her seat to give Brenda a hug.

Michael was standing beside Brenda as she gave Celine a hug.

"Hello," said Michael.

"Hello, you're welcome. What can we do for you?" asked Celine, as she mistook Michael for a client.

"Oh, sorry, he's with me. Please, where's John?" asked Brenda.

"John will be out of Tom's office in a minute," said Celine. In his usual fashion Michael decided to introduce himself formally to Celine. "I'm Michael, and you're...?" asked Michael.

"Oh, Celine," she said. They looked at each other with keen interest as they shook hands after the formal introduction, and Celine returned to her seat after her handshake with Michael.

"What about Philip?" Brenda asked.

"Philip is fine; he went out and will be back soon," Celine replied. Brenda's visit is a vivid reminder to Celine that winning John's heart is now a lost battle, and sadly, Celine is now a princess waiting for her own prince charming that she'll eventually turn into a toad.

Moments later, John walked into the open office as he stepped out of Tom's office. "Hey baby, you're here," said John.

"Michael, this is John, my John," said Brenda.

"I'm Michael. Nice to meet you, John," said Michael. John stretched out his hand for a handshake with Michael even though he wasn't expecting a guest he knew nothing about in the person Michael. Brenda stood between the two men as she makes a formal introduction.

"Michael is a high school classmate, we stumbled into each other a few weeks ago," said Brenda.

"Brenda is a very good girl, please treat her well. I told her I would like to meet you," said Michael. "Oh, I never knew Brenda had an old school mate that cares about her this much. She's in a safe hand, I promise," said John, with a smile. John and Michael chatted for a while after they've been formally introduced.

"Michael, you've seen John, we need to get going," said Brenda.

While Brenda and Michael were about to make their way out of the office and in a surprising turn of events Michael walked up to Celine.

"I'm leaving now, but can I've your card? I'll give you a call," said Michael.

Celine was taken aback by Michael's bold move, but seem to like his confidence.

"Hmm.., my card?" asked Celine. She immediately reached for her bag and found none, and after rummaging through her top drawer, Celine brought out her card and handed it to Michael.

"Ok, thank you," said Michael.

Michael could not stop thinking about Celine since they shook hands, it was as if Celine reached out to Michael's soul through the handshake. Moments later, while John walked Michael and Brenda to the car, Michael stopped suddenly.

"That lady, Celine, how is she?" asked Michael. The question about Celine came to John as a surprise, but he knows that this question isn't about Celine's gender or what role she performs in this law firm, it's much more than that.

"She's a nice lady with a good heart, fun to be around and she doesn't sleep around," said John.

"Please, John, are there other things I need to know about her?" Michael asked curiously.

"She will make you laugh and her sense of humour is best described as wit and surreal," said John. Brenda and John were taken aback and gobsmacked with Michael's sudden interest in Celine and the new line of questioning that followed. He continued his quest for Celine's profile, and sadly, Brenda likes surprises but this one from Michael doesn't fit what she considers a good surprise.

"Is that the reason you became fixated on her the moment you set your eyes on her?" Brenda quarried.

"I saw her and felt it would be nice, if I knew her better," said Michael. Brenda's protest isn't about Michael's interest in Celine but an attempt to protect her flawless reputation before John. She felt the need to prove to John that the good friend she has just brought to meet him isn't some creepy kind of guy.

"She's undoubtedly a good looking woman but this isn't the reason I brought you here," said Brenda.

"I'm serious about settling down, and stumbling into a good looking lady whose facial expression represents kindness means a lot to me," said Michael.

"You should've told me you wanted to meet Celine, before bringing me here so you could meet her," Brenda retorted. Unsurprisingly, Brenda didn't see providence playing a big role in this, and she remained confused as to how Michael could serendipitously come to see John for a handshake, only to find Celine.

"This wasn't planned, and I didn't know of her existence before now, just trust me," said Michael.

Michael tried to tone things down, as he tried to assure Brenda that his meeting with Celine was nothing but providence and told them of his desire to pursue his interest in Celine further. This whole drama suddenly left Michael on the back foot, as Brenda reminded him she hopes he wouldn't want to be seen as jumping to many fences at once because that's exactly what his action is saying.

Sometimes the consequences of our actions follow us around, and more often than not the consequence is just there waiting for us at every turn we make, and grappling with the expected surprise from our past could be quite scary. Celine on the other hand didn't suffer any consequence from her messing about with John, thanks to John's benignity. That night while Celine settled into the sofa with a remote in her hand after having her dinner, her phone rang.

"Hello, this is Michael," he said.

"Err, Michael, do I know you?" asked Celine.

"I was in your office earlier today with Brenda," said Michael.

"Oh, you're the Prince Charming that came calling in my office today! She exclaimed.

"Yeah, it's me," said Michael.

"Ok, how're you doing? I never expected you keep your word," said Celine. Michael sounded very lively on the phone and didn't spend time trying to choose his words. His big personality was on full display, even though he tried to be as modest as much as he could in his conversation with Celine. This isn't false modesty of some sort, neither is he illusory, Michael has decided to get it right this time by fitting into Celine's mould. It's arguable that the vagaries of life meant we never can tell what life has in store for us.

"I do keep my word, and the truth is, I like you and I want to marry you. What do you think?" Michael asked, paying keen attention to his phone to hear what Celine has to say.

"Oh my God, marry me just like that! Celine exclaimed.

"Yeah, just like that, though it sounds like a fairy tale," said Michael. This surprise move by Michael swept Celine off her feet, and she's now trying to find her balance, so as to hold a sensible conversation. It was quite obvious to Michael that Celine almost jumped out of her skin the moment he mentioned marriage.

"We don't know anything about each other, and you're talking about marrying me? This sounds so weird to me, Michael," Celine retorted.

"Our story can be like the fairy tale of two people who stumbled into each other, fell in love, married immediately and then lived happily ever after." Michael said, laughing.

"We don't know each other well, Michael. That might mean we could end up not living happily ever after," said Celine.

"I suppose you're aware that the length of courtship, doesn't determine the success of a marriage," Michael said.

"Ok, but we need to sit down and talk, because I don't sleep around and I take marriage seriously," said Celine.

"Tomorrow, I'll come and pick you up for lunch," Michael proposed. Celine is mindful of the unnecessary attention that might be precipitated by Michael's visit. She thinks it might create some sort of unspoken rivalry, and a lunch date, a day after they stumbled into each other might be too brazen and make her look cheap.

"Err.., I'll suggest we make it a dinner date instead," said Celine.

Michael paused for a while, as he steers the conversation away from mere pleasantries.

"Please, what do you hate the most?" asked Michael.

"I'd hate to marry a duplicitous man. What about you?" asked Celine.

"I must confess, I'd hate to marry a nagging wife," said Michael.

"It's already late; we'll talk about this tomorrow," said Celine, with a big smile on her face.

"Ok, dream about me, said Michael. They chatted for a while and then wished each other good night.

Celine and Michael meet for a dinner date after work, which was their first time alone together, and interestingly, Celine went for the vegetarian option, as her main course.

"Oh, I like this vegetable paella. It tastes nice," said Celine.

"That's why I brought you here, it's because I know you aren't used to this," said Michael.

This spot is a bit different from the regular cafes Celine usually hang out, this cafe is overwhelmingly for the middle class, as per demographics, the cafe looks more like a place where the middle class commune. While they had their meal, the Karaoke bar which was just by the corner within the cafe was busy entertaining them.

After having their meal, they continued catching up, and Celine stood up abruptly and whispered into Michael's ear saying she has a special song for him, wondering what she's about, she then told him she's going to the Karaoke bar to sing a track. Michael asked what track it is she has in mind, she whispered again and said it's all a secret and it won't be nice letting the cat out of the bag prematurely.

Michael laughed and watched as Celine walked to the Karaoke bar and requested a turn. It didn't take long Celine began singing the track "Santa Baby" by Eartha Kitt.

Santa baby, just slip a Sable under the tree for me Been an awful good girl Santa baby, so hurry down the chimney tonight.

Santa baby, a 54 convertible too, light blue I'll wait up for you dear Santa baby, so hurry down the chimney tonight

Think of all the fun I've missed Think of all the fella's that I haven't kissed Next year I could be just as good If you check off my Christmas list

Santa baby, I want a yacht and really that's not a lot Been an angel all year Santa baby, so hurry down the chimney tonight

Santa honey, one little thing I really need The deed to a platinum mine Santa baby, so hurry down the chimney tonight

Santa cutie, and fill my stocking with the duplex and checks Sign your 'x' on the line Santa cutie, and hurry down the chimney tonight

Come and trim my Christmas tree With some decorations bought at Tiffanys I really do believe in you Let's see if you believe in me

Santa baby, forgot to mention one little thing A ring, I don't mean on the phone Santa baby, so hurry down the chimney tonight Hurry down the chimney tonight Hurry, tonight

She performed the track so perfectly well in a manner that got Michael so delighted in a special way. Michael suddenly stood up and went for her while she still had the microphone in her hand. He then held her hand and they repeated the chorus of the song one more time. Michael loved Celine's bravery, and that was the watershed moment that made him come to the conclusion that this is the woman of is dream. Celine on the other hand was particularly delighted that she was so much loved by this Prince Charming that came calling just a day ago.

She now suddenly came to the realisation that while she was busy trying to find herself a man, life on the other hand had a package in the person of Michael waiting for her.

The pair received the accolades of other customers in the cafe who were lavishly entertained, and it didn't take long before they returned to their seat to continue with their catching up.

The moment they took their seat, Celine hinted Michael that even though this isn't Christmas, he likened him to her Santa. Michael adjusted his seat, and held her hand.

"Tell me about yourself," asked Celine. "My mum is still alive, my dad has passed away but I'm single, and never married. I worked in Canada with an oil firm, and we're opening a new branch here in London, and here I am," Michael said, as he delivered his profile.

"Ok, never married! Celine exclaimed. Michael is jovial, good looking, quite interesting to be around, and has a good job. Celine is convinced that Michael has everything that will surely make women like to be with him, so, she's thinks there might be some baggage spilling from his past relationship even though he's never married. "What about your ex-girlfriends? I do hear stories of exes lurking in shadows, and I don't want any surprises," said Celine.

"One ex-girlfriend, but distance separated us, and she's now in another relationship," said Michael.

"You know my name, what else do you want to know?" asked Celine.

"I made some enquiries about you, and I must confess that you're highly recommended," said Michael.

"Ooh, now I know, it's John that told you about me, and I'll kill him," said Celine, as she burst into laughter.

"He mentioned the qualities I needed in a woman, and I must confess, you're exactly what I wanted," said Michael. "What are the qualities you desire?" asked Celine.

"You've a good heart, fun to be with, you don't sleep around, and you take commitment seriously," said Michael.

"Err, you mean John said all this!" Celine exclaimed. Michael paused for a while, with his eyes fixed on Celine, he then smiled and without wavering or vacillating he went straight to the point. "Will you please marry me?" asked Michael. "Yes, yes, but this looks like a fairy tale to me," Celine said as she burst into laughter.

Michael then slipped an engagement ring into her finger, then proceeded to say "I bet my life, you'll not regret this, and I want to take you to the altar," Michael Promised.

"What's the plan about that?" asked Celine. Michael never had the urge to get married but since he stumbled into Brenda, he felt this sudden sense of urgency to get married, and he was like a child on a sugar rush.

"Can we join John and Brenda to make it a double wedding?" asked Michael.

"What? It's like you had this all planned out before coming to me, and it's like John put you up to this," Celine protested.

"No, it was providence that brought us together and I'd no idea of your existence before yesterday," said Michael.

"Two weeks isn't enough to plan for anything, John and Brenda have been together for nine months, so your two weeks won't work," Celine retorted. Michael became momentarily silent as he tries to work things out in his head. "Let's try to speak with John and Brenda and see how they react. I understand the cold feet, and there's no need for that unless you're in doubt of my person," said Michael.

"I'm not in doubt, my hunch tells me to trust you, but I don't know why," said Celine.

"I'll speak to John and Brenda, and if fate is on our side it'll work out," said Michael.

Michael is moving ahead with things, and nothing seems to be stopping him, particularly now that he has got his own woman by his side. He then thought it wise to discuss his plans with John and Brenda. This time he decided that the spot with the right ambience for such conversation will be to meet up with John and Brenda in their usual spot for lunch break. He got there just as John and Brenda finished their lunch, and headed for their car. After a brief exchange of pleasantries, Michael hinted them that he proposed to Celine and she accepted. He was quite enthusiastic, with his hands in his pocket.

"When did that happen? I know you only met her two days back," asked John.

"But isn't this too quick, and who proposes to a woman within 24hrs of stumbling into her?" Brenda retorted.

John isn't overly taken with fussing and nit-picking on the intentions of others, he really didn't like the situation this time, but he remained calm and collected as he tried not to make the situation any worse than it already is.

Brenda muttered inaudibly saying she will do whatever she can to stop this idiotic move from going ahead even if it involves waterboarding Michael because she thought Michael was having a laugh but she soon came to realise he isn't.

The barrage of questions coming from Brenda didn't make it any easy for Michael as he tries to wriggle his way to their hearts. "Length of courtship doesn't determine a successful marriage," said Michael. John was taken aback with the twists precipitated from his encounter with Michael, and fears that things are getting creepier by the minute, but has no qualms about Celine finding true love in Michael.

"Celine is a good girl. Please, I don't want you to hurt her in any way," John pleads.

"You don't know me, but she knows me and I'm not that kind of guy," said Michael.

"Michael is decent," said Brenda as she gave a boost to Michael's profile. Michael knew the next line of conversation wouldn't only be creepy but enough to blow the hats out of everyone's head, and will certainly be a hard nut to crack. Yet, he decided that there's wisdom in approaching the matter cautiously than being straight on point as he often does. Sometimes there's no logic to this, and things don't always line up straight as they should but this time it's quite a different kettle of fish.

"When I say what I have in mind, please don't say I'm stupid," Michael pleads, as John and Brenda seems lost with this new line of conversation.

"What do you have in mind?" asked Brenda.

"Can we make the wedding double? You and Brenda, Celine and I," asked Michael.

"Wow, Michael. That's creepy!" Brenda exclaimed, and she didn't know when she muttered asking Michael what's it he's smoking that will make him make such a request.

"Where does this idea come from? It isn't a wise one," said John. Michael stood before John and Brenda looking stupid and lost for words, yet continued to press his views home.

"I know it's a stupid proposition but I want to marry as soon as possible," said Michael.

"But why the hurry and what stunt are you trying to pull?" asked Brenda. Michael can't take back what he just said, the genie is out of the bottle and can't be put back. It's now embarrassingly obvious that Brenda finds this move to be insanely surreal, and her panoramic understanding of this whole thing might mean they've a hell of a rollercoaster ride ahead.

"Please, you guys could make it possible. Make this sacrifice for me," Michael pleads.

"You're a friend but this is too much to ask," said Brenda.

"The priest won't accept getting involved in this convoluted arrangement," John retorted.

"Ok, allow me to speak with the priest to see how things will pan out," said Michael.

This elephant in the room can't be overlooked, and despite blowing hot, Brenda subtly persuaded John to allow Michael try his luck with the priest, John accepted Brenda's proposal but someone needs to connect Michael to the priest.

"Hello Father. It's me, Brenda," she said.

"How're you, Brenda, and how's John?" asked Father Bill.

"Father, I'm fine, but is it possible to do a double wedding at the same time?" asked Brenda.

"We do it, but the individual couples have to go through separate counselling," said Father Bill.

"These are our friends and their dream is to have their wedding the same day as us," said Brenda.

"The church doesn't just wed people, I need to speak with them and assess their Christian faith," the priest insists.

"We'll study those books together, though Michael is here, let him answer for himself," said Brenda.

"Hello Michael, are you a devoted Christian?" asked Father Bill.

"Yes, I'm a Christian, but not devoted as you may expect, but I'm ready to live my life for God," said Michael. Unsurprisingly, the priest knows too well not to allow people use him to mess with God but the sincerity in Michael's response was encouraging.

"Good to hear you promise to live for God and you know it's not right to tell lies to God," said Father Bill.

"Father, this is a dream I look forward to. Please help me make it happen," Michael pleads.

"You've to come with your fiancée within the week, so I can have a word with both of you, to see if that'll be possible," said Father Bill.

The day after Michael's convincing conversation with John and Brenda, Celine walked up to John as he sat at his desk and then stood in front of him.

"Thank you, John," said Celine.

"Thank you for what?" asked John.

"For the good things you said about me to Michael, you played the role of a good friend," said Celine. "What are friends for? I told you, you're still my best friend," John said, with a smile.

"The next set of drinks is on me," Celine promised, with a whispering tone.

"The fact that you made advances to me doesn't mean you do that to others, and I've never seen you mess around," said John.

After receiving the much-needed green light from Father Bill, Michael and Celine paid a quick visit to Yorkshire to seal their wedding plans with the priest. The priest welcomed them, and asked them to make themselves comfortable. Celine on the other hand was encouraged by the manner in which Michael dropped his big personality and assumed a modest posture in the priest's office.

"Marriage is a serious life-long commitment that doesn't require any rush," said Father Bill.

"Yes Father, and I know God is against sex before marriage, so we want to do the things right," said Michael.

"Are you both ready to give your lives to Christ? Giving your life to Christ is about commitment," Father Bill asked, looking straight into their eyes. The priest didn't hesitate to put every artificiality aside as he laid bare his position in the matter, and interestingly, the soon-to-be couple are willing to go the whole hog to get this right.

"Yes, we are," they both replied. After a period of intense conversation and counselling, the priest led them to Christ, and then handed them books on the importance of a lasting marriage and how to achieve it.

"Make sure you read them, and I'll ask you questions from these books," the priest assured.

Immediately after spending time with the priest being counselled, Celine didn't even wait to get back to London before informing her mum that her wedding bells are by the corner and already ringing. While still in the church premises, she called to inform her mum of her wedding.

"Mum, I'm getting married! exclaimed Celine.

"Oh, at last my daughter is taken. Who's the lucky man?" Beth asked, in an ecstatic tone.

"His name is Michael and he just relocated to London," said Celine.

"What does he do? Do you love him?" asked Beth. "Of course, I do love him and he works with an oil firm. Though, not a fat cat, but he's well to-do, and well-mannered," said Celine.

"When is the wedding taking place?" asked Beth.

"25th October," said Celine.

"So quick? That's less than two weeks from now!" Beth exclaimed.

"Everything is happening so fast, Mum. And I don't want to lose this opportunity," said Celine.

"I'd love to meet him" said Beth. "Ok, we'll come over to yours by the weekend," Celine promised.

The moment Michael and Celine left the priest, and while Celine was some feet away speaking to her mum, Michael picked up his phone and informed John of Father Bill's approval of their intention to wed alongside them. Interestingly, Brenda was by John's side when the phone call came.

"How did it go, Michael?" asked Brenda. "It went well, the priest approved our wedding, and I just want to say thank you," said Michael.

"Meaning, we'll need to meet to plan together," John proposed.

"We'll do our best to make sure the wedding is successful," Michael promised. Brenda muttered saying Michael's promise to do his best isn't good enough, rather he should promise doing whatever it takes to make the wedding a success.

"We'll come over to yours so we don't mess things up for you, and we equally want to succeed as well," said Michael. After her phone conversation with her mum, Celine joined Michael who had just ended his phone conversation with John and Brenda and waiting some distance away.

"I told to my mum about you," said Celine.

"Oh my God, what did she say?" asked Michael.

"She would like to meet you, and I've promised her we'll see her over the weekend," said Celine. This whole wedding thing is still like a dream to Michael, even though the rush was his idea, the whole thing is more like a rollercoaster as opposed to a fairy-tale. "Ok, I'll be there, but I want to ask you a question before we take this further," said Michael. "What question?" Celine asked anxiously.

"Are you convinced in your heart that I'll make a good husband?" asked Michael.

"I don't think I need a shrink to make me believe in you, and I don't know why, but I trust you," Celine assured Michael. Celine's response didn't steal Michael's thunder, but it did bring about this sudden realisation that Celine has put her fate in him. This isn't just because he's some sort of scruffy intellectually improvised wreck but for posterity's sake. Even though he's sincere in his love for her, he's keen to know Celine believed him as someone who could make her happy, and she isn't swayed by his big personality.

"I suppose, you remembered what I said about giving my life to God," said Michael.

"What about it?" asked Celine.

"I meant it, Celine. I've always done things my own way and things haven't always panned out the way I'd wanted. I have the personality, the looks, the charm and even fun to be around but things haven't always worked as planned. Father Bill touched my life strangely, and from now, I want to lean on God completely to see how he leads me," said Michael.

"I'm not used to this, but I'll equally join you in this journey of leaning on God completely," said Celine.

They then decided to give in to studying the word of God, and the books on marriage given to them by Father Bill, so God can guide them in this new journey called marriage. Michael was predictably delighted that providence was on his side as his life choices suddenly fell into place.

By weekend Celine visited her mum to formally introduce Michael to her mum.

"Mum, meet Michael. I mean, my Michael," said Celine.

"Oh, you're Michael, how're you?" asked Beth.

"I'm fine, and nice meeting you," said Michael. While Michael settles into the sofa, Celine left Michael with his mum as they chatted following their formal introduction. Moments later, Celine returned with a bottle of Chardonnay and three glasses as she gave Michael a glimpse of her mum's hospitality.

"My name is Elizabeth but my friends call me Beth, my daughter said a lot of good things about you," said Beth, holding a glass of wine.

"Celine is a wonderful lady, her friends have said so many nice things about her," Michael replied, as he looked at Celine and smiled. Celine interjected and said thanks to John, who said those nice things about her, she proceeded to describe John as a gentleman. They all burst into laughter.

"I learnt your wedding is coming up 25th October?" asked Beth. Michael interjected while Beth was still speaking. "And it is going to be a double wedding, we just want to do it and get it over with," said Michael.

"Don't worry, we've started preparations already," Beth said, assuring Michael in a very ecstatic tone.

"Thank you for assisting us despite the short notice," said Michael.

Now that the wedding date is set and the bells are about to ring, Celine has one more bit of tidying up to do, and that involves informing Tom Bradley about her fast approaching honeymoon that must happen after her wedding. Her next day at work, she decided to address this mater head on, she then invited Michael to her office to formally introduce him to Tom Bradley.

"Tom are you busy?" asked Celine. Tom lifted his face to hear what Celine has to say.

"Do you want to see me?" asked Tom. "Yes, this is Michael, my fiancé," said Celine.

"Ooh, this is good news and it's a step in the right direction. Do you live in London?" asked Tom.

"Yeah, but I'm new here. I used to live in Canada, but my office is opening a new branch here in London," said Michael.

"He works with an oil firm that recently moved to London," said Celine.

"You're welcome, Michael. I suppose you know my name already, I'm Tom, and just keep me informed of your plans, Celine," said Tom. Tom then turned his attention back to the file he was working on before the interruption, but Celine has more than mere exchange of pleasantries in her mind.

"That's why I've come to see you," said Celine.

"Ok, go ahead, said Tom, as he lifted his face again to attend to Celine.

"Our wedding is fixed for 25th October," said Celine. Celine's comment must have struck a raw nerve to provoke a stern reaction as Tom's countenance changed immediately.

"What! 25th of October, the same day as John? You should've told me about this earlier," Tom protested.

"It's going to be a double wedding and we didn't know about this date earlier than this." Michael interjected.

"Is this double wedding going to be at the same venue and time as John and Brenda's wedding?" asked Tom. After a moment of silence, Celine and Michael stood statue-still in front of Tom. Arguably, this information obviously left a bad taste in Tom's mouth. It was obvious to Celine and Michael that this news that was meant to be a good one seemed to have spooked Tom. For what it's worth, Tom isn't a man waiting to pile up enough pennies before allowing his employees to tie the knot, he's just being a businessman.

"Ok, we'll talk about this later," Tom retorted.

The moment Celine and Michael left Tom's office, and headed towards the car park, Michael didn't hesitate to poke holes in Tom Bradley's reaction to the news of their wedding as Celine walked Michael to his car.

"What was that all about?" Michael asked as he attempts to enter his car. Celine looked around to see what Michael was talking about.

"What are you talking about?" Celine asked.

"Didn't you notice a change in his countenance immediately you told him of our wedding date?" asked Michael.

"I suppose he's concerned about who will be left in the office to do his work," said Celine.

"He's supposed to be reasonable with us on this," Michael retorted.

"I know Tom to be a very good man, and I hope he'll be considerate with us," said Celine.

Michael then decided to leave the matter alone, and said, since Celine said Tom is nice, and reasonable, he will also consider him to be a nice man as well.

"Ok, bye," said Celine, she then gave Michael a hug as he entered his car and drove off to his office.

Michael was quite upfront as he breaks the news of his engagement and wedding with excitement to his mum who has always pestered him to get married because she would like being called "Nana" but Michael hasn't given her the privilege to earn that title.

"Hello Mum, how're you?" asked Michael.

"I'm fine, Michael, it's just my back that's killing me," said Lillian.

"How bad is it, mum?" asked Michael.

"It's bad enough, because it's troubling me," Lillian replied. Michael's good news had to wait until his mum's health issues are addressed. Unfortunately, his mum's reoccurring back pain has dampened his mood as his ecstatic frenzy disappeared immediately he got on the phone.

"Have you gotten any medical care?" Michael probed further.

"Yes, I went to the doctor two days back, and I was able to go to work with it," said Lillian.

"Mum, you've got to slow down, there are younger people working with you in the library," Michael emphasised.

"I'm not that old, I'm just sixty eight, Michael. Why're you sounding as if I'm old?" Lillian protested. Lillian is young at heart, she epitomises age as a mindset. She doesn't like being told she's old even though her body no longer cooperates with the youthfulness of her heart. Lillian still pushes herself on a daily basis doing things the under twenties do, and unsurprisingly, she steered the conversation away from her health but Michael wants that matter addressed.

"But you've got to consider your back, so it won't continue to hurt you," Michael advised.

"How's London? Have you been able to buy the property you were searching for?" asked Lillian.

"I'm yet to find a property. Mum, we've other things to talk about," said Michael. Michael knew her mum too well, and knows for sure that she would want to meet his fiancée even before he makes the decision on whether to marry her or not.

"What's it you want to talk about?" asked Lillian.

"Mum, I'm getting married," said Michael. "You mean you're getting married? I must say this is the best news I've heard in the last ten years," said Lillian.

"Whatever you say, Mum," said Michael.

"How is she? and what does she look like, the colour of her eyes? I know you like ladies with blue eyes," asked Lillian.

"You're right, mum, about the colour of her eyes, does the colour matter?" asked Michael.

"I'm only curious about what my daughter-in-law looks like, and what's her name?" asked Lillian. After breaking the good news of his wedding, Michael knew that his next comment will rattle his mum's cage, yet he went on, though with a bated breath.

"Her name is Celine, and the wedding has been fixed for 25th of October," said Michael. Lillian got hopping mad at her son's insensitivity in a manner that left her reeling from within. "You've fixed a wedding even when I've not spoken with her, not even through the phone?" Lillian yelled.

"She isn't here with me right now, but I promise you she will speak with you tomorrow," Michael promised.

"But 25th of October is just about ten days from now, Michael. Am I so insignificant that you're telling me about this now?" Lillian yelled again, as she expresses her infuriation.

"Mum, it wasn't planned, we met not long ago, and I felt we should get married immediately, sorry if you feel slighted but it's all happening so quick," Michael pleads.

The next day after the close of work Celine went straight to Michael's place as they further their wedding plans, but Michael has a more important matter to resolve and that's introducing Celine to his mum.

"What drinks do you have at home?" Celine asked as she walked into Michael's apartment.

"I've got red wine, tequila, and brandy, what's your pleasure?" asked Michael.

"You know what, Michael, since we visited Father Bill, I've cut down on alcohol" Celine retorted. She opened the refrigerator and reached for the fruit juice to help sooth her appetite.

"Our spirits seem to be working alike and I've never tasted spirit since our meeting with the priest, except for the glass of chardonnay your mum offered me. It's like Father Bill did something to my soul," said Michael.

"We've taken this our newly professed faith seriously, said Celine, as she pours herself a glass of juice.

"My mum wants to speak with you," said Michael.

"Oh my God, that'll be wonderful, please give her a call immediately!" Celine exclaimed. Michael stood up and reached for his phone and dialled his mum's phone.

Interestingly, Lillian quickly dispensed of all pleasantries immediately she answered the call and asked about her soon to be daughter-in-law.

"Is Celine there?" asked Lillian. Michael handed the phone to Celine.

"Hello, Mother-in-law," Celine said. "Hello Celine, please call me Lillian," she said.

"Ok Lillian, how're you doing?" asked Celine.

"I'm fine, my son told me about you," Lillian said.

"Yeah, sorry I haven't called you before now," Celine apologised. Michael knew his mum hates being left in the dark when it comes to important life's decision such as him getting married, bringing his mum on board at this point might require reinventing the time machine to help bring her up to speed.

"I told Michael I'm disappointed, but you're forgiven," Lillian retorted.

"We're very sorry about how you feel. It isn't long since I met Michael, and the whole thing just went so fast," said Celine.

"He said your wedding is just nine days from today," Lillian asked.

"Of course, Lillian, but we want you to know that no one can take your place as far as the wedding is concerned," Celine assured Lillian. To make this insult less painful, Celine had to patronise her mother-in-law by way of assuring her that she matters a lot to her.

"Ok, I'll speak to you before then, at least to know how to support you and Michael," said Lillian.

"Ok Lillian, thank you," said Celine. After speaking to Lillian, Celine passed the phone to Michael to conclude his conversation with his mum.

"Mum, I'll speak with you tomorrow but I'm making every arrangement for your comfort," said Michael.

Beth was in high spirits as she prepares for her daughter's big day, but she was held back by the thought that the caterers aren't yet on board and decided to give Celine a call to discuss why the caterers aren't brought in early enough.

"I'm calling to ask you about your plans," said Beth.

"Mum, we've got things under control," said Celine.

"You've got just one week to your wedding, what about the food and drinks?" asked Beth.

"No, Mum, there won't be any cooking, and after the church service every guest will go straight to the hotel where they'll be entertained," said Celine, as she assured her mum she's got everything under control.

"Oh, that'll be good, said Beth.

"The reception will take place at the hotel, and the hotel will also take care of the food and there will be a variety. The guests will enjoy themselves," said Celine. Beth was already anxious and all over the place as she prepares for her daughter's big day. Though, worried about the level of preparation, she's now constantly on the phone trying to assist in getting things ready but Celine has to allay her fears by letting her know that things are under control. "I'll send some money into your account so you can shop for the wedding," said Celine. Beth was ecstatic the moment her daughter mention shopping. Shopping is Beth's hobby and this is another opportunity for her to shop till she drops.

"My daughter wants me to look good on her wedding day. What about Michael's mum, have you spoken with her?" Beth asked anxiously.

"Yes, I have. She will be here the day before the wedding," said Celine.

"Where do we stay on that day? Beth asked further. "I'll book accommodation in the hotel for my guests, and it'll be perfect," Celine promised.

Celine had gotten no definite response from Tom Bradley who told her they'll talk about their wedding plans later after briefly introducing Michael to him. Time is now of the essence as the wedding date is drawing near and Celine has no plans to quit her Job, and yet, doesn't want her wedding plans to go up in flames.

It's now eight days to the wedding, Tom Bradley called John and Celine to his office the moment they resumed for the day's business. "I called the two of you into my office to discuss your wedding plans and how it affects our job in the office," said Tom.

"What about it, Tom? I think we've concluded on that," asked John. Tom concluded with John when Celine wasn't in the picture, with Celine's wedding and honeymoon plans thrown into the mix that makes the whole thing to indeed be a pretty kettle of fish.

"Yeah, but with Celine having her wedding the same day, I don't think it'll be fair to this firm," Tom retorted. Tom Bradley isn't used to being put in a situation where he feels he isn't in control of what goes on in his firm. It's like, instead of the dog wagging is tail, the tail is now embarrassingly wagging the dog this time, and he's having none of it.

"Tom, it's just a wedding, and it isn't the end of the world. We'll be back," John assured. Tom was beginning to get more agitated by the minute as he tried to bat away the misconception that this wedding has nothing to do with their jobs. He was about to let rip as the conversation with his employees lingers. John now finds his boss insufferable, because he could sometimes be cold and cranky, and this is sadly one of such moments, and yet he's the go-to-person in this office. Tom's perception of a double wedding is a different beast and this meant he isn't going to let the request for leave by Celine and John at the same time fly.

"Who will do your jobs, when both of you're gone for your honeymoon? I'll get two people to replace both of you," said Tom, as he looked straight into their eyes.

"That isn't fair, Tom. We've been with you and these weddings matter to us," John protested.

"You can always get a job, you're qualified enough to get a new one as soon as you're ready," Tom said, in an unusually soft-spoken voice.

"Tom, you don't have to do this," said Celine, who's now becoming emotional over Tom's stance.

"Celine, this is happening because of your sudden decision to wed in just eight days' time," Tom retorted.

"Tom, please rethink your decision. If there's any time we need you most, that time is now" said John.

All pleas from Celine fell on deaf ears as Tom sidestepped their sweet talk and went straight for the hammer. Sadly, Tom isn't just a hurting acquaintance who'd enjoy spending time with John and Celine, he's their boss, and a businessman for that, and his business mustn't suffer. For all it's worth, Tom Bradley understands that this wedding meant a lot to Celine and John, and yet will never acquiesce this joyous moment sounding the death knell to his firm.

After much back and forth, John and Celine left Tom's office looking depressed and exasperated as they returned to the open office. Fortunately, Philip and Lesley weren't in the office at the time.

"John, I'm very sorry about all this, Celine said, with a feeling of guilt.

"Actually, I knew it would come to this," said John.

"You knew?" asked Celine.

"Yes, this isn't a government establishment, this is a private firm and what do you expect! John exclaimed.

"But I never expected Tom would take things this far," said Celine. Tom's heavy handed reaction shattered every of Celine's glimmer of optimism that things will work out as the whole thing seem to be coming down on Celine in a manner that seems to take the wind out of her sails.

"He doesn't want his firm to suffer, he's only protecting his business," said John.

"Then what do we do now?" Celine asked, as her feet remained glued to the floor and her hands fiddling with her hair, which is what she does unconsciously whenever she's troubled.

"Let's give him a few days to get used to the news, I think it's too much for Tom to take in," said John.

"John, I'm so, so sorry about this," Celine apologised.

"Don't worry, it isn't your fault, and you deserve to be happy as well." John said, as he tries to calm frayed nerves.

"John, please, let's keep this between us for now," Celine pleads.

"Away from Philip and Lesley?" asked John.

"No, away from Michael and Brenda, I just don't want Brenda to see me as a spoiler," said Celine.

"Ok, I'll do just that," John promised.

John's relationship with Celine is best described as an epitome of happy memories and for all it's worth, John worked so hard to salvage his friendship with Celine, and he hopes to keep it that way.

Concerned about his history with Brenda, Michael decided to visit Brenda in a show of appreciation, but was accosted by David who thought Michael has come to close a deal on the property he was looking to buy.

"Good to see you, Michael. What's up with your bank?" asked David.

"You spoke with my bank?" Michael asked curiously.

"Yeah, but they're too slow for my liking," said David. Michael turned to Brenda after the brief conversation with David. They stepped outside the office to avoid interruption with their wedding plans. Michael began by thanking Brenda for playing the adult in the room, the moment he proposed the double wedding to John. Yet he assured Brenda that his perception of Celine is that she's in no way a scrounger and has no intention of taking him to the cleaners in the near future or anytime in the future because her interest in him is rock solid.

"You're right, let's avoid awkward moments," said Brenda. After putting his fears to rest, Michael then steered the conversation back to their wedding plans, and promised to transfer sixty percent of the total wedding expenses into Brenda's account later that same day.

By the close of work the next day Tom Bradley invited John and Celine back to his office, after making their blood run cold from their previous conversation.

"Your actions aren't justified, even if you read your handbook you'll see that you've not acted in line with this firm's polices of giving notices, but I'll not stand in the way of your happiness," said Tom. Sadly, Tom's comment unwittingly left John and Celine lost as his words didn't convey any decision concerning the quagmire they find themselves.

"Please, Tom, what does that imply?" asked John. "I've slept over what we talked about yesterday and felt I should consider you guys," said Tom. Celine understands that John's case was settled but things went south the moment she got in to the mix.

"Which of us are you considering?" Celine asked curiously as she could barely justify her decision to choose the same wedding date as John.

"I'm considering both of you," said Tom.

"Thank you very much, Tom," John said, with excitement.

"Tom, thank you. This confusion came up because of me and the truth is, I just found love after a long wait and I don't want to miss this opportunity," Celine said, in a low and emotional tone.

Tom isn't just a boss in fancy pants, he's good at what he does, and has got a mind like a steel trap, and funnily, this conversation isn't about who first give the other a bloody nose. John and Celine looked helpless as their boss decides their faith. Tom Bradley then decided to call in some favours from a friend who could cover while these two are away, but had to first make his intention known.

"Celine, you'll have to prepare a written handover note and transfer all the case files in your custody to Lesley," said Tom.

After an exhilarating meeting with Tom, John and Celine were elated to get things back on track as they plan for their double wedding. Now that a possible kerfuffle with their boss is out of the way, all roads now leads to Yorkshire where John and Celine will make their vows. The hysteria of a double wedding didn't make things any easier either and Celine's mood is emblematic of a lady caught up in anything but a pre-wedding depression. Interestingly, a day to the marriage, the domestic guests are on hand while guests coming from abroad had to go through the rigours of airports checks and be checking into their hotel rooms so they could rest their feet after a long and tiring trip. Celine was excited to meet her soon to be mother-in-law as she and Michael awaits the arrival of her flight at Heathrow Airport on her arrival from Canada for their wedding that's happening a day away.

Moments after the plane touched down, Michael stood holding hands with Celine as he anxiously awaits his mum in the arrival lounge.

"Ahh, that's my mum," said Michael as he points to his mum.

"Is that her coming? You know I haven't met her before," asked Celine.

"Of course, that's my mum," said Michael as he rushed to get her luggage.

"Welcome, Lillian," said Celine.

"Oh my God, Celine, is that you!" Lillian exclaimed.

"Yes, Mother-in-law, it's me!" Celine exclaimed.

"You look so beautiful. How are you?" asked Lillian. The ecstatic reception Lillian received at the airport sets her off with joy and her weariness of heart disappeared immediately.

"I'm fine, it's good to finally meet you. Don't worry, when all this is over, I'll come to Canada and spend two weeks taking good care of you," said Celine. Lillian turned to Michael who's standing by the side as Celine and Lillian exchange pleasantries.

"Michael, you chose correctly, I like her and she's beautiful," said Lillian.

"Mum, we're going straight to Yorkshire, I've booked a lovely room for you," said Michael.

"Lillian, are you hungry? At least you need to eat before we continue," asked Celine.

"No, I ate on the plane and the meal was nice. I liked it," said Lillian. They all headed to the car park, but Michael followed his mum and Celine from behind and watched his mum and wife-to-be chat as if they've been friends forever. He was particularly glad that there was an instant connection between his mum and his wife-to-be.

"Mum, have you witnessed a double wedding before?" asked Michael.

"You told me it's a double wedding but I haven't attended one before," said Lillian.

"At least you'll have an opportunity to take part in one," Michael assured.

That same evening while preparations were in high gear, John and Brenda went to Heathrow Airport to receive Sharon, her husband Kane, and Reverend Karl and then drove them straight to the hotel booked for them in Yorkshire. Fortunately, it was the same hotel Michael's mum was lodging, and while Sharon and her husband made their way through the lobby, there was a flicker of recognition as she spotted someone that looks like Lillian.

"Isn't that Lillian, Michael's mum! What's she doing here?" Sharon asked, the moment she approached the reception area of the hotel.

"Of course yes, Michael is wedding tomorrow as well?" said Brenda.

"In a different church or the same church?" Sharon asked.

"It's the same church and in fact it is a double wedding," said Brenda.

"Seriously, and you never bothered to tell me? I'm coming, let me say hi to Lillian," Sharon said.

Sharon quickly negotiated her way through the busy reception area, and went to Lillian whose sharp eyes recognised Sharon as she approached, they hugged each other and the pleasantries followed immediately. Brenda didn't hesitate to join the party. After all, it's been long since she saw Michael's mum.

"Hello Lillian, how're you? I'm quite surprised to see you," said Sharon.

"Oh my God, Sharon, is that really you? And this is Brenda, I suppose. It has been quite a while," Lillian said, as she gave Sharon and Brenda hugs after the first hug. Seeing Sharon and Brenda sent Lillian down memory lane and Lillian's heart was flooded with wonderful memories as she became teary and emotional.

"Sorry about your husband, Brenda told me he passed away," said Sharon.

"Jay is gone, he passed a year ago, said Lillian.

Michael came to the reception area from the lodgings only to see his mum and Sharon exchanging pleasantries and hugging each other endlessly.

"Hello Sharon," said Michael as he stood beside Sharon laughing. "I saw you the other day and you never told me you were getting married," Sharon protested.

"Sorry, it happened so fast, and I don't want Brenda to leave me behind," said Michael. Lillian turned to Brenda and held her by the hand as the conversation was going on.

"Brenda, are you here for Michael's wedding?" asked Lillian.

"No, I'm wedding tomorrow as well, said Brenda.

"Oh my God, you're the other couple that's wedding tomorrow, did you and Michael plan this?" asked Lillian.

"No, it just happened," said Brenda. "Though, it's good to see you, and I'm happy for you," said Lillian.

Moments later, Michael turned around and saw his cousin, Nate, approaching the hotel reception area. "Oh my God, Nate, you came to England?" Michael screamed, as he rushed towards Nate. "I told you nothing in the world will keep me away from your big day!" exclaimed Nate.

"And you kept your word. How did you know of my big day, because I can't remember telling you about it?" asked Michael.

"Was my being in the dark deliberate, or unintended?" asked Nate.

"Ahh, I can't keep news of this nature away from you, but the circumstance surrounding this event is different, and I hope you'll forgive me," said Michael.

"Your mum told me about it, and the circumstance as well, so you're forgiven," said Nate. With Nate's eyes flickering, he then whispered to Michael.

"You're forgiven only after the groom shows me his bride," said Nate.

"It just happened, and I seized the opportunity, come with me please," said Michael. They both walked towards Celine who just took some steps away from Lillian towards the bar.

"You must be Celine?," asked Nate.

"Of course, and you're my guest, I suppose?" replied Celine, as she looked at Nate with Keen interest, thinking he must be one of Michael's relatives. Michael interjected and held Celine by the hand.

"Celine, meet my cousin, Nate. We call him the Alamo," said Michael.

"Ooh, Alamo! Does he have anything to do with the state of Texas?" asked Celine.

"He was born in Texas, close to the Alamo mission" said Michael.

"Nate, nice meeting you, and thank you for coming," said Celine. Alamo as his friends and relatives call him, is some kind of guy that lightens up their space, and his encounter with Celine isn't an exception.

"Oh my God, you're pretty, and you guys are perfect for each other," said Nate.

"Excuse us, Celine, let me show Nate to his room," said Michael.

"Ok, see you around, Nate," said Celine.

Wedding Ceremony

All the guests sauntered in one after the other, and it didn't take long, the guests for this auspicious occasion were all seated and all the topsy turvy is now in the past. Philip stood right beside John as his best man, and Michael's work colleague, Holmes stood by his side. The grooms stood statue-still and waited anxiously as both brides walked in one after the other, and the ambience was nothing short of memorable.

It didn't take long before it was time for the vows and kisses.

John: I, John, take you Brenda to be my lawfully wedded wife, to have and to hold, in good times and in bad times, in sickness and in health, from this day forward. I give you this ring as a symbol of my love and faithfulness to you.

Brenda: I, Brenda, take you John to be my lawfully wedded husband, to have and to hold, in good times and in bad times, in sickness and in health, from this day forward. I give you this ring as a symbol of my love and faithfulness to you.

You've declared your consent before the church, I now pronounce you man and wife. You may now kiss the bride," said Father Bill.

Then the priest turned to Michael and Celine, and asked them to repeat after him.

Michael: I, Michael, take you Celine to be my lawfully wedded wife, to have and to hold, in good times and in bad times, in sickness and in health, from this day forward. I give you this ring as a symbol of my love and faithfulness to you.

Celine: I, Celine, take you Michael to be my lawfully wedded husband, to have and to hold, in good times and in bad times, in sickness and in health, from this day forward. I give you this ring as a symbol of my love and faithfulness to you.

You've declared your consent before the church, and I now pronounce you man and wife. You may now kiss the bride," said Father Bill.

They threw their bouquets to the crowd and both couples left the reception for their honeymoon. John and Brenda travelled to the Caribbean Islands for their honeymoon, while Michael and Celine travelled to Spain for their honeymoon. And both couples lived happily ever after.

Books by Boniface Ossai